'I killed for you, Slattery,' said Sol Rim, 'make me a rich man or I'll see you hung.'

Slattery dug his hands into his coat and came out with a sovereign. At once Sol Rim's eyes glistened and he smacked his lips. 'Why,' said Slattery softly. 'You would grovel for this, even now.' He dropped the gold to where it lay glinting in the grass. 'It's yours.'

Sol Rim looked from the coin to Slattery and back again. With a grin he stooped forward.

In one terrible, shuddering movement Slattery raised his stick high in the air and brought it crashing down on Sol Rim's head . . .

Witness

DAVID JOHNSTONE

Illustrated by
Anthony Maitland

A Magnet Book

For Elizabeth,
Esther and Emily

First published in 1983
by Methuen Children's Books Ltd
under the title *Redemption Greenbank*
This Magnet edition first published in 1988
Reprinted 1989
Michelin House, 81 Fulham Road, London SW3 6RB

Printed in Great Britain
by Cox & Wyman Ltd, Reading

ISBN 0 416 07462 6

ONE

He was expected. The crazy wooden gate of the cemetery stood half open. Jacob Slattery paused and fretfully swished his stick at the tall weeds that grew rank along the path. The long walk from town had brought a glow to his cheeks and perspiration to his brow. A fool's errand, he told himself, a waste of good shoe leather. He peered inside. As dismal a collection of urns and stones as most men would walk miles to avoid - who in his senses would make an appointment here? There was no business in old stones and old bones. He'd half a mind to throw the whole thing up and go back to his office. But he dare not, that was the truth of it. It was a message he could not ignore.

A well-to-do man, Mr Slattery, sleek and portly, decently dressed in black, something of an old woman but with another quality that lurked occasionally in the corners of his eyes: ruthlessness, perhaps.

The cemetery was disused and dismal. The merchant appeared to be looking for something; he studied the sepulchral figures of stone angels with a particular attention. Here, one knelt, another raised a finger to heaven, yet another stroked a harp. They didn't satisfy Mr Slattery who carried on, in his timid way, further into the heart of the cemetery. Once he started, thinking he heard a movement; as he wiped his hands with his handkerchief he called out -

'Are you there?' There was no answer, only small birds fluttering in the yew.

At length his path led him to a clearing which was dominated by one monument, an angel with a broken sword. This was the limit of the cemetery. Behind was wilderness, long grass, bramble and a dilapidated hut which the grave-digger had used to store his tools. Two benches were set down for the convenience of visitors and behind them in the bank were one or two rabbit buries. The area was liberally spotted with droppings and the grass short and cropped. None of this was noticed by Slattery who stared hard at the monument and impulsively reached for the scrap of paper in his pocket –

> 'Meet me in the old berying ground near the Angel with the broken sword I Know about Sarah'

Mis-spelt, crudely executed, its meaning was plain enough. Slattery closed his eyes for a moment, trying to ward off the sensation of nausea which had been rising in him ever since his clerk had handed him the note that morning. He had come as soon as he dare.

Suddenly he became aware that he was being watched, that he had been for some time. He turned to see a man lounge towards him from the shadow of the yew.

'You came, Mr Slattery.'

Slattery's mouth was dry, his tongue worked to free itself.

'You haven't forgot me.'

Sol Rim. The pinched narrow face flecked with grey about the jaw like an old wolf. Sol Rim. Once pointed out to him as a man who would do any deed for money.

'I haven't forgotten you.' He had thought of him every day. 'It is almost ten years. I haven't forgotten –'

'Come, Mr Slattery, have I been haunting you?'

'Yes.'

'Well I'm here in the flesh now – leastways what there is left of me. They've been ten thin years for me, precious thin. But now I've found your hidey-hole.'

As he said this Sol Rim eyed Slattery and smacked his lips almost as if he was going to eat him.

'I think I must sit down.' Slattery did not even bother to wipe the bench clean. 'Why have you come? Why did you use *her* name?'

'Your wife? Well, we both know she's dead enough, but I

thought if I said her name you would be sure to come.'

'Yes.' Slattery sighed. 'Well here I am. What is it you want – money I suppose?'

'Money and a lot of it too. I have been looking a long time, Slattery and I have a wife of my own to support. She laughs when I say I could be rich but she don't know what I know. Why should you live rich when I live poor? Look at me.'

He looked little different to the first time they met; more ragged, but the yellow teeth were the same, the same cruel reflection in his eyes.

'I've come many miles finding you, Slattery. You're a long way from home.'

'I wanted to get away.'

'You've done well for yourself too. Quite a person you are in this town. Brass name-plate, ships sailing in and out of the harbour, there's a lot of fat on you one way and another.'

'They're not my ships.'

'Aye, but they carry your stuff – I've seen 'em loading and unloading. Why, there isn't a man stands as high as you when it comes to loading and unloading.' Again Sol Rim smacked his lips. 'I want some of it,' he said.

'What do you want?'

'Five thousand pound.'

Slattery's face worked itself into a fearful grimace somewhere between a grin and an expression of loathing. The first impulse was to laugh wildly, he controlled it with difficulty. As he did so he felt a great dark weight settle on him.

Sol Rim repeated his demand. 'Five thousand pound, Mr Slattery. It ain't beyond your means.'

'Five thousand pounds would ruin me. It's a nonsensical figure. I'll give you ten pounds to leave the area.' It was an effort to sit erect. He was trembling.

Sol Rim thrust his face into the merchant's. 'Mister Slattery I'm a desperate man.' His breath was foul. 'I don't want your ten pound! I done a murder –'

'Not so loud!' Slattery looked about wildly.

'I done a murder for you. I killed an innocent young wife –

don't think it don't lie heavy on me because it do – I want paying proper Slattery. Not the fifty pound you paid me afore – why, I can drink up fifty pound in a month if I've a mind! I've a woman to keep that laughs at me. We live in one stinking room in the Seven Dials and every time I'm away she slides off. I want respect! I want paying proper – I took a life. Make me rich for it!'

The merchant struck the ground with his stick. 'We both know what happened, don't speak of it! Where's the other one? You had a friend, he has to be paid too, I suppose.'

Sol Rim showed his teeth. 'No, he don't. He's dead. Bowers was his name and he signed a confession afore he coughed it. It's safe with me. At least it's safe if you pay me what I ask.'

A spasm of panic twitched across Slattery's face.

'Come on Slattery – you always was too much of a woman. You can't stand up to me. I'm a leech, I'm a bloodsucker. Pay me the money and be rid of me.'

'A confession?' Slattery felt weary, hopeless. 'You can't blackmail me for a kill – for something you committed.'

'There ain't no mention of me in this document. Bowers shouldered the load hisself afore he went off to tread the streets of Glory. And it's legal – stamp on it, witnessed, everything. You pay me my money Slattery, or I shall go to the law. They shall hear of all the tricks Jacob Slattery, late of Putney in the county of Surrey, got up to afore he come north to Wellshead.'

'Five hundred pounds ... five hundred pounds for this document and that is more than I can afford.' Slattery stood up and leaned on his stick. 'I don't have business enough to sustain such a loss. I will go to my office now. You have your teeth in me ... I expected you for a long time.'

'I do! I'm a reg'lar terrier, Slattery! No, I'm a bloodsucker, I won't have none of your five hundred pound – I want five thousand, that's the figure I'm set on. I'm going back to London in a coach with a bag of money. I've come to grind you, Slattery. Grind you and flay you.'

'Where did you conceive of such a figure? Do you want me

to cease trading? Do you want me to sell up? Five thousand pounds is ruin to me. Ruin!'

'Do I care?' Sol Rim grasped a handful of his own tattered coat. 'Look at me, I sleep in ditches and barns. Look at me, Slattery! No better than a dog while you live soft and sleep soft. I killed for you, Slattery – make me a rich man or I'll see you hung.'

Slattery dug his hands into his coat and came out with a sovereign. At once Sol Rim's eyes glistened and he smacked his lips. A look of contempt replaced the fear on Slattery's face.

'Why,' he said softly. 'You would grovel for this, even now.' He dropped the gold to where it lay glinting in the grass. 'It's yours.'

Sol Rim looked from the coin to Slattery and back again. With a grin he stooped forward. 'The first of many, master.'

In one terrible, shuddering movement Slattery raised his stick high in the air and brought it crashing down on Sol Rim's head. It was enough.

TWO

'Lord have mercy on us all. Amen,' muttered the boy, high-kneeing it hurriedly up the hill past the cows. At the crest of the hill he glanced around, as if he feared pursuit, and only paused long enough to spit to the four winds and murmur some rhyme or charm. This done he pushed himself beneath a gap in the hedge and onto the open road. He was wearing a charity uniform which in these parts meant only one thing; he was an inmate of McMurdo's. He was, in fact, Redemption Greenbank, named by the late matron of McMurdo's, Mrs Fletcher, who was a Puritan of the old school. His surname came from the parish he had been born, or rather found, in.

He hurried on down the road, glancing back at the gazing cows, muttering every scrap of prayer he had retained from Mrs Fletcher's bountiful provision.

The orphanage looked baleful in the gloom of evening but the boy entered like a swallow homing. He flung himself through a side door and careered down the corridor.

'Ah wouldn't be thee, Red! She's looking for thee!' 'She' was the new matron, Mrs Biggs.

Ignoring the comments of the other children Redemption picked up a broom and hurried to his place of work.

A pale boy, Redemption, as he swept the yard outside the laundry. In his mind's eye the stick arced through the air; in his ears the sound of wood on bone. It was a judgement; he should never have cut school to visit his snares. Poaching was wrong too – two wrongs in one day. If he had stayed in with the others he would be happy now. What was it that made him continually seek his own solitary path?

Work was supposed to be done in silence but he heard the usual muffled giggles, the careless clatter of buckets wielded by those of light heart. It would have been better for him to have been born an animal. The cows in the field near the cemetery didn't care about what had gone on. And he, dunderhead, why had he stayed to listen to the two men? None of it was his business. He hadn't understood the half of it until the heavy stick had come crashing down on the ragged man's skull and blood had splashed the tombstone. He shouldn't have been there. He ought to tell but no good ever came of telling.

His brushing, which had become mechanical, paused at two feet and bombazine skirts. Mrs Biggs, nunlike, cold as a winter morning, surveyed him.

'Redemption.'

'Yes'm.'

'Mister Blaney tells me you weren't in school.'

'No'm.'

'Where were you?'

'Laking, ma'am.'

Mrs Biggs shook herself and her keys jingled softly like a rosary. 'Look at me, child.'

Redemption lifted his eyes to her face, noting again the faint smear of whisker on her upper lip before he met the wintry eyes. He hated Mrs Biggs worse than he had hated Mrs Fletcher. She had a way of looking at him as if he was something nasty the dog had brought in. He didn't know she was ashamed of herself, believing herself to be socially above the position necessity forced her to.

'By which reply I take it you were roaming the fields, wasting your time. What were you doing?'

'Snares 'm.'

Another shake. 'A common poacher! I wonder whose blood runs in your veins, Redemption.' A sour smile. Wherever did Mrs Fletcher get these ridiculous names? Plain John and Sally was good enough for her. 'Still we mustn't enquire too closely into that now, must we? One can guess only too well at the stock from whence you spring!'

'Ah's not afeard of thee, anyhow,' muttered Redemption.

Mrs Biggs reserved a special dislike for this spiky child, she never quite felt in control when dealing with him.

'I wonder what sort of woman your mother was,' she said spitefully.

'A foolish one,' returned the boy.

The foolishness of their parents in allowing the inmates of McMurdo's to be born at all was a constant theme with Mrs Biggs. The frost on her face melted slightly, 'Indeed. Why was she so foolish?'

'In leaving me anywhere near this place,' replied Redemption shortly.

Mrs Biggs took hold of his cheek between her thumb and forefinger and pinched hard. The boy did not wince but, gratifyingly, his eyes filled with tears.

'You are a bold, insolent boy!' Her breath was coming fast now, 'You infect everyone about you with your defiance, your stupid, wooden manner, your constant disobedience.' Her gaze took in all the watching children, 'Truly, this is a stiff-necked generation! But I will bring you all to heel.' To Redemption, 'No supper. Come to my room when the meal is over.'

And he knew what that meant. At eleven or twelve he was getting too big for a woman to beat satisfactorily but Mrs Biggs tried hard enough.

'You will learn obedience, Redemption Greenbank if I have to raise a welt on every part of your body.'

She swept away. Redemption watched her go, restraining a sudden impulse to fling his broom at her head. McMurdo's would not keep him much longer.

Supper at the orphanage never held any surprises as it normally consisted of what was left over from dinner with the extra addition of water. A visitor might experience some disquiet at the scummy soup known as potato stew but the inmates had no such inhibitions. They watched each portion hungrily as it passed down the table. As Redemption was doing without there would be extra tonight. The news that a draped corpse had been seen being carried from the cemetery only added zest to their appetites. Inspector Trumper, it was said, was there in person, looking every inch the fool he was.

A certain body of opinion held that the Low Road Boggle was at work; others that a gang of cut-throats had fallen out while dividing ill-gotten spoils. All agreed that Inspector Trumper would never sort it out.

'I don't rightly know what he *was* doing,' observed Henry, who had been among the crowd of urchins held back at the cemetery gates by a uniformed constable. 'He weren't looking for clues - not that I could see. He was pacing up and down. Up and down, muttering to hisself like a man trying to remember summat. Then he starts to whistle a tune. Then - strike me dead if I lie - he stands on one leg. Addled, see.'

Henry scratched his head with his spoon and dropped his voice to a hoarse whisper, 'They brung in buckets of water.'

There was general puzzlement at this.

'Blood!' Henry hugged himself with demonic glee, 'They had to clean up, see!' He nudged Redemption who sat, pale and silent, at his elbow. 'Think of the blood, hey Red?'

Redemption shut his eyes. He could see the blood, hear the blows as they rained down.

'Thou knows nowt, thee,' he said bleakly. 'Talk about something else. Leave us alone.'

Already the wind had begun to insinuate itself around the orphanage, shaking the bushes, rattling gently at the windows. Most of the children began to think it would be a good idea if they dropped the matter altogether. They respected Redemption, he was his own man and if he wanted to brood on his forthcoming appointment with Mrs Biggs, well, they could understand that.

He had made up his mind to tell the matron. It would be a long night and every time he closed his eyes there would be the stick in its arc through the air, the awful sound of the blows, the expelled hiss of breath after each one, the blood splashed on the stone. He would escape a beating too.

* * *

Mrs Biggs ate alone. So stiff and unbending was she that it was difficult to imagine her at this activity. Tonight a pork chop and a good portion of potatoes and greens were consumed in a grinding manner as she stared fixedly at nothing. She ate alone, lived alone, ran the orphanage and its staff in a remote, severe way that avoided unnecessary personal contact.

Her late husband had left her nothing, perhaps as revenge for their life together. She had been forced to find an occupation that provided both upkeep and shelter. How she loathed it!

Hers was an empty room; long silences broken only by the clock ticking, the rustle of her garments, a sigh.

Tonight there was a boy to be beaten; it was a humiliating task but it allowed her to give vent to the sour feelings of the day which she could taste, like bile, in her mouth.

He was not late. Redemption presented himself at the appointed time, a compact, spiky-haired boy with a steady gaze. He glanced at the cane in her hand in an indifferent way. She always used a cane, a tawse needed a man's hand to be effective.

'Well . . .' She felt disposed to talk. She knew he would take his beating sullenly; she would be no nearer breaking his spirit. Abruptly she brought the cane down on the horsehair chair, raising a dust.

'Are you afraid of me, Redemption?' she demanded sharply.

'No, ma 'am,' said the boy with the same infuriating air of indifference.

'You are unnatural. You *must* fear me,' she said, fiercely, 'Has not God given us the spirit of fear that we may learn and obey? Are you sorry? Do you feel sorrow, you unnatural child?'

'Sorry that I cut Mr Blaney's school this afternoon? Aye,' Redemption replied huskily, 'I am sorry for that. I am sorry too that I went poaching. I done two wrongs and have been paid for it. I never knew so much harm could come from trying to take one poor rabbit.'

Mrs Biggs' grasp tightened about the cane; she had the

uneasy suspicion he was attempting to deceive her but could not see how.

'Can I believe this? Is this contrition?'

'Yes ma'am,' whispered Redemption.

'Well,' she let out her breath in a sigh of pleasure, 'after sorrow comes punishment. Lower your breeches.'

He did not comply.

'Redemption.'

He ignored her, frowning, then suddenly made up his mind and spoke.

She was on the alert for deceit but as she listened she sensed he told the truth. She put by the cane reluctantly and sat down.

'Tell me what you saw.'

He could see no compassion there but only a rapt greedy attention. A glow enlivened her eyes making them like coals in the gloomy room.

'Tell me . . . hurry . . .'

'There's rabbits gets down there where it's all wild and tangled and folk will pay a few coppers for fresh rabbit . . . I like to sit in t'old hut . . .'

He told it all. When he had finished he was conscious of a small relief. She was not looking at him.

'Ten years,' she was saying softly. 'Yes, ten years that would be right. It was said he was unlike our homespun worthies, a finicky man. Womanish, you say?'

'T'other called him so.'

'Jacob Slattery . . .' In her eyes was a faraway, speculative look. 'I wonder . . .'

She dismissed Redemption with stern injunctions to silence. Her excitement was mounting and when he had gone she paced the room restlessly.

'Jacob Slattery . . . Jacob Slattery.' Then, 'It would be worth the attempt – I will go out!'

The long room was warm with the breath of sleeping children. Outside the wind hurled handfuls of rain at the windows and sent a slate crashing into the yard below. It was good to be abed. There was a salt tang to this wind. It came straight from the sea roaring like a bully, buffeting everyone, tearing down branches from the trees, shaking the windows. It could all be enjoyed in bed. If McMurdo's knew contentment and pleasure, it was in this room.

Redemption shifted to his back, listening to the wind and the occasional mutterings of the sleeping orphans. The village boys often tempted him to try some night-time poaching. Pheasants, they said, could be knocked over and bagged in the time it takes to blink. Then there was the long net, the gate net, the hares. His mouth watered at the thought of it all but in order to enjoy it, he had to sacrifice the only peaceful and quiet time in his life. So far he had been unable to do it.

Soon he would be free of McMurdo's. They couldn't keep him for ever, they would have to apprentice him out before long.

He became conscious of a gradual illumination in the room. A figure, bearing a taper, was walking between the two ranks of beds. As she drew nearer he saw it was Mrs Biggs; a different Mrs Biggs with her hair let down, her face full of shadows.

'Get up and dress,' was all she said. She was wearing a loose night-gown which billowed slightly in the draught.

He stared up at her.

'I have found someone to take you. After what you told me last night I think it better you leave us – the associations of that dreadful event . . .' Her voice trailed away, 'Hurry.'

There was a lamp lit in the big kitchen where all the cooking pots were set, clean and empty, the lamp winking back from them. The door was open on the night; outside the wind tore at the trees sending leaves hurrying across the floor.

'This is Mr Factor.' The leaves scurried about his boots like mice, a tall man in a greatcoat, his hat slouched low over his face.

'Eat your breakfast.'

So it was morning. They watched him eat and drink without a word. Mr Factor sat leaning against a corner of the stove. Mrs Biggs stood with her lips pursed and her hands clasped together, restraining herself. She was nervous, wanting them to be off.

Redemption wiped his mouth with his sleeve. 'What time is it?'

Mr Factor stood up with a creaking of his boots and signed that they should go. Mrs Biggs brought out the lamp to where a horse stood tethered. Redemption was swung into the saddle.

'Hold his mane.' Mr Factor mounted behind him and with a clatter they were away.

Redemption had a last glimpse of Mrs Biggs, her grey hair hanging loose, her gown billowing.

There was a moon to see by and the elms tossed their heads as they passed. Flurries of rain stung his face but Mr Factor offered him no shelter, merely slouching his own hat lower over his face. The clouds streamed above them as if making for an assembly over the hills inland. The road passed the scene of yesterday's murder, the white stones gleaming in the moonlight. Redemption shifted his eyes to the horse's ears and to take his mind from the afternoon began to think about where he was being taken. Mr Factor offered no clue; his dress was plain and could belong to any number of callings. The horse was a pretty beast and must have cost a penny or two. He patted its neck, thoughtfully. Stable boy? There were worse jobs. He hated McMurdo's and he hated Mrs Biggs - good riddance to the both of them. Wherever he went couldn't be much worse.

They rode for a mile or two beneath the hurrying clouds, making all the time in the general direction of the sea. Then, as the moon hid behind a dark mass in the sky, they left the road. They were on some sort of driveway, the thick rhododendron on each side plunging them into black night. Factor spurred on more quickly, breaking into a canter, they were almost home.

As they rounded the curve of the driveway the moon came out from behind the cloud again. Before them stood a massive square house, every part of it bathed in ghostly light. His new home. Were they to make a servant of him then?

Factor dismounted and led him indoors.

Still Factor spoke no word. He picked up a lantern and took Redemption down a narrow passageway, the lamp shedding so little light that the boy had to grasp his coat. A small door opened and they were in a spacious, high-ceilinged hallway. The staircase was wide enough to drive a coach and four up it.

Factor prodded him upstairs. By the light of the lantern he saw only dark walls and deeper shadows but his nostrils were filled with a musty carpeted odour. Mister Factor was a rich man then.

As they reached the first landing he heard a door being opened downstairs.

'Thank you, Factor.' Standing in the doorway, the light of the room coming from behind him, was the man from the cemetery.

'The new member of our household. Take care of him.' He looked like a man who had not slept all night. 'I bid you welcome.'

He advanced towards them.

'We must look after him.' As he approached from the shadows his eyes were unnaturally bright.

'Look at me.' He took the boy's face in his hands, 'Do you know me?'

His hands were soft and smelt disagreeably of soap.

'No,' said Redemption, swallowing, 'I never saw you before in my life.'

'You are a poor liar, sir,' whispered Slattery. He shot a glance at Factor and turned away, putting a hand on the banister. 'We will decide what is to be done later,' he said, with his back to them.

Factor led him up more stairs and then yet more; their footsteps sounding hollow as carpet gave way to bare boards.

As the lamplight slid along the damp walls Redemption's eyes were wide with fear.

He knows I saw him, he thought. I'm as good as dead.

THREE

Inspector Trumper, chief of the Wellshead police force – a sergeant and two constables – leaned forward over his desk with an expression of concentration.

'Aleph, beth,' he muttered, 'gimel, hoth no – *heth*, oh Lor!'

He sank back in his chair as his assistant entered. 'Put some more coal on the fire, would you sergeant?'

When his sergeant returned, red-faced from bending at the fire, the inspector observed, 'I'm taking lessons in Hebrew from the vicar. I can't even remember the blessed alphabet. It's all my wife's idea, she says I need intellectual stimulus. I was once intended for the Church, did I ever tell you that? Before I disappointed my father.'

The sergeant grunted. Everyone knew Inspector Trumper was an odd fish, gentleman turned policeman. His open face and guileless manner made most people think him a fool. The sergeant didn't.

'About this body, sir.'

'The vicar was telling me that St Jerome was brought close to despair over Hebrew, can't blame him.' The inspector was leaning on the mantlepiece now, turning his head this way and that to admire his sidewhiskers in the glass. 'Did you ever hear of a language without vowels?'

'The body, sir,' interrupted the sergeant patiently.

'The body? – ha! Yes, that's what turned me to Hebrew. On the score of the body my mind is as empty as the bottom drawer of my splendid desk. Normally with a case of this nature in Wellshead we have a round dozen of witnesses come forward to say they heard the row if they didn't actually hold the coats. I don't mind telling you there's something hole and corner about this business. The man's completely unknown.'

'There's someone here now, sir.'

'Good Lord – there you are. Still, we haven't had a nastier cadaver in the mortuary since that boy fell from the cliffs last year. Who is it – did he do it?'

'Hardly sir, it's Mr Slattery.'

'Slattery?'

'You know him, sir. The merchant with offices in Scotch Street. He lives up in the old Ridler place – the big house that overlooks the harbour. I expect he likes to watch his money sailing in and out. He won't have a woman near the place, they say, he has the one man to do it all.'

'Odd chap,' murmured Trumper. 'He wouldn't enjoy my home – not with my wife and daughters in such evidence. What does he want?'

The sergeant looked aggrieved. 'Wouldn't say exactly. Saw the report in the paper and wants a word with you.'

Trumper was flattered. 'Mustn't keep him waiting, sergeant.'

Slattery was pale but as smartly dressed as ever. He carried his hat and stick.

'Allow me,' Trumper busied himself with the courtesies. When Slattery had removed his coat they both sat down on either side of Trumper's massive desk. Slattery's jowls glistened sleekly and a faint smell of perfume came from him.

'We seldom have the pleasure,' murmured Trumper. 'What can we do for you, Mr Slattery?'

Slattery cleared his throat. When he did speak his voice was surprisingly soft.

'I saw the item in the *Free Press* this morning about the murder. You are reported as asking anyone who may be able to help with the identification of the body to come forward.'

'Yes, we've had one or two people in. Apparently the fellow was seen about the docks for the past day or two. No one knows who he was and he avoided all opportunities for conversation. Blessed nuisance the whole thing – I'll be frank with you, Mr

Slattery I want to get the whole affair cleared up by Christmas. Have you come to shed a great light, ha?'

'A little,' Slattery studied the polished surface of the desk. 'You see, I was passing the cemetery yesterday afternoon.'

Trumper reached for a pad, 'Time?'

'About three, I think. I was on my way to the orphanage – something to do with a boy I'm helping.'

'Lucky little fellow.'

'Yes. As I say, I was passing the cemetery.'

'You were on foot?'

'I walk whenever I can.' Perhaps Trumper was not the imbecile popular report made him out to be. He must be wary.

'I loathe exercise myself. I would have thought you kept a carriage.'

'I believe we have a contraption somewhere. I am rarely abroad. I walk whenever I can. I am pedestrian by nature.'

Trumper smiled a polite disclaimer.

'Indeed. It is by plodding, by taking first one step and then another that one gets on in business. We have none of your excitements.

'When I passed the cemetery I saw two men loitering there –'

'Aha! Now we have it. You can describe them?'

'They were both ragged, ruffianly fellows. You will understand that I did not study them but I recall that one was tall and bearded – they were both tramping – the shorter man was older. He was unshaven, he was grey ...' Slattery shrugged. That was enough to be going on with.

Inspector Trumper drummed his fingers on his desk and whistled between his teeth. 'You realise the importance of this evidence, Mr Slattery? The greybeard was murdered and you have probably seen his murderer. Your testimony will be required before the coroner and if the case comes to trial you will have to repeat it before a judge.'

'I understand.'

'Very good. My sergeant will take your description of the two men – particularly the taller one – and in due course will prepare a statement for you to sign. Meantime –' He drummed his fingers and regarded Slattery.

'We have a grisly chore.'

Slattery's eyes widened imperceptibly.

Trumper watched him. 'You and I will have to identify the body. The mortuary – known as the "dead house" – is not, I'm afraid, adjacent to this building. We will have a little walk together – a great pity as I had intended to have a morning before the fire. Unlike yourself I have a deeply-rooted objection to fresh air. It was delicious being in bed last night during the storm was it not?'

As he chatted Trumper was thinking what an odd, pent-up fellow Slattery was. Why, the thought of viewing a corpse seemed to excite him. 'You have no objections?'

'No – no!' It was what he had come for. All night the image of Sol Rim had stared his mind almost out of countenance. He must see him again, if only to ensure that he was truly dead.

The wind had abated a little, although now the sky was crammed with heavy, grey cloud. It was a day made for misery but as they walked Trumper kept up a flow of good-humoured chatter, apparently unperturbed by the monosyllabic answers he received.

For his part Slattery was reflecting how one small evil could compound so many others much greater. It was like a business contract, one clause led to another in succession. He had married not for love but for money, respect, position. Once married he could not suffer it, so cloying and intimate was it. When the money was his he had no further use for a wife. Her death was, on the face of things, the only real escape. The secret part of his youth had been spent in a search for excitement that took him beyond the bounds of respectable society. He had no difficulty in contacting Sol Rim. He had been out when intruders broke into his house . . .

'Here we are.'

They entered by a door set in the wall. The 'dead house' was like a small brick cottage with its windows walled up. The smell when they entered was odd and as the door swung to after them Slattery was startled to see a heavy apron hanging there like a sentinel.

'He's in here,' said Trumper, in a matter-of-fact way, as if they were visiting an invalid who was sitting up in bed.

Sol Rim lay on a slab covered in drapery. The sheet was not long enough so his two bare feet stuck out, pale and bloodless.

Trumper twitched back the cover. 'There are heavy contusions to the face consistent with the fact of his being beaten about the head with a blunt instrument. Taking all that into account, can you positively identify this person as one of the men you saw?'

The jaw was open and the one undamaged eye stared straight at him.

'What - are you ill?'

Slattery's mouth worked.

'Dead! Yes ... dead!' It was a harsh, triumphant sound. He gazed a moment longer, his features working as if he were making faces at the corpse, and then turning he flung himself from the building.

'Damn.' Trumper stared thoughtfully after Slattery. 'That wasn't what I asked at all. I know he's dead.'

He was dead. Even though the gaze from that one lifeless eye had burned him to the soul, he was dead. Outside, in the cold air, he felt better. It could have been dangerous, his compulsion to gaze on the results of his work, but Trumper seemed unconcerned.

'It has an awful reek, that stuff they use to stop the body ... er ... going off.' He patted Slattery on the shoulder and recommended brandy and milk with a scrape of nutmeg as the best restorative after the horrors. He took his leave, advising Slattery to keep out of the wind, and promising to get in touch at a later date.

Slattery had other business. He walked to McMurdo's and, as he waited to speak to Mrs Biggs, the doorkeeper asked after Redemption Greenbank.

'We hear you've took young Red, Mr Slattery. 'Tis to be

hoped he's properly grateful – mind he's a handy lad. What's ganna be done with him?'

'The sea,' said Slattery drily, after a pause.

'Virginia trade? Aye, well we shan't be seeing much of him then. Tell him we sent our best for his future days. I always liked young Red, I hope he won't forget his old friends.'

When he was alone with Mrs Biggs he turned upon her sharply.

'You have told everyone that I have the boy?'

'Yes,' Mrs Biggs opened her desk. 'Here are the necessary papers. Sign them and you become responsible for him. He need speak with no one. Send him far away – you have complete authority.'

Slattery signed, while the ink was drying he passed over an envelope which he took from his pocket.

'As we agreed last night. Take this draft to my bankers and they will pay the amount in full. They will observe the utmost discretion.'

Mrs Biggs hastily glanced at the paper before locking it away.

'I need hardly add,' continued Slattery, 'that I presume this to be the end of the matter.'

Mrs Biggs nodded. 'Have no fear, Mr Slattery, you will hear no more from me. My price is low is it not? I shall leave this place. If you only knew –' she continued in an undertone, 'Oh, if you only knew how I have longed to leave. How I have prayed for an opportunity –'

'You have taken your opportunity, I think.'

'Why not?'

'You become a party to crime.'

'Call it crime – what harm is there? What could make that miserable child's life more miserable than it is already? I have your word you will not harm him.'

'You believe me?'

'You are not a common criminal.' She glanced at him. 'You are a gentleman.'

'We make a pretty pair.'

Mrs Biggs cut him short. 'That is all. You will hear no more from me.'

Women, reflected Slattery as he was shown the door, were disgusting creatures. Mrs Biggs had heard the boy's story last night and had seen at once how the affair could be turned to her own advantage. There had been no pause, no softening impulse, no sympathy. His fear that she would not fulfil her part of the bargain was quite gone. Last night, as she stood in his drawing-room the rain glistening on her cloak, he had thought her determined. Now, in the cold light of day, he was doubly sure: determined and heartless.

He adjusted his gloves and shivered. How much evil was there in everyone? Jacob Slattery, double murderer, surveyed the winter landscape and shivered not with cold but from the sense of evil all about him.

Inspector Trumper was warming his back at the fire, leaning on the mantlepiece.

'Normally I enjoy a steak and kidney pudding,' he was saying, 'but my appetitie is quite spoiled today. Take it away sergeant, eat it yourself. Couldn't touch a mouthful.'

The sergeant picked up his superior's steaming plate. 'Thank you, sir. I don't mind if I do. A man can eat two dinners when the weather's as keen as this. Give you a turn did he?'

'I'll say he did. Dashed odd the way he regarded that cadaver I'll tell you something, just between ourselves, I had the distinct impression he was gloating. Just imagine that pudding was the corpse he –' And Inspector Trumper did his best to reproduce Slattery's facial expression.

The sergeant paled and put down the plate. His appetite too was diminishing.

'What do we know of our friend Slattery? Gossip, anything?'

'Little enough, he's not talked of.' The sergeant furrowed his brow. 'He come up from the South and had money when he come.'

'Ah yes, the South. You forget sergeant that I am not

unacquainted with that distant clime myself.'

'Yes, sir, we all know you are a university man.'

The inspector was admiring his profile in the mirror. 'Once an Oxford man always an Oxford man,' he murmured, 'even if I was sent down. You say he has no staff in the house?'

'One man – Christian Factor – we know nothing against him. He come in from the villages some years ago. Dull and stupid but he does all there is to do. It's believed Slattery can't bear women.'

'How odd – I believe I'm what is known as a ladies' man.'

'Yes, sir.'

'It's true, I am. However, we must do some police work. Circulate the description Slattery gave us and . . .' Trumper looked meditatively at the floor, 'set in train some discreet enquiries about Jacob Slattery. Let not your left hand know what your right hand doeth.'

'That's dangerous ground, Inspector. What purpose would it serve? He's a rich man. There would be an awful row if he got wind of what we were doing. There's no sense to it.'

'Do it, all the same.' There was a determined note in Trumper's voice. 'Most of the population think I'm a fool – hey?'

The sergeant blushed.

'Don't answer that – you have a good heart and I hate to see a man lie. But I'll tell you this, I saw two things in Slattery's face today. He knew the man –'

'How would someone in his position know a ragged tramp?'

Trumper shrugged. 'How indeed – bear with me, sergeant. Scratch about. I am fully aware that there is no motive, or murder weapon, or witness. I realise that if we say a word out of place to a man of his means we may well end up in the dock ourselves on a libel charge.

'Good Lord, if we were dealing with the criminal classes here I would hale him in now and accuse him of it – just to see what his reply would be.'

'You said you saw two things, sir. What was the other?'

Trumper's reply was perfectly sober. 'Evil.'

FOUR

That day the first thing Factor did was to bring him a complete change of clothes; green jacket, grey breeches, thick grey socks, black boots. The shivering boy handed over his McMurdo's uniform as the servant waited wordlessly. The new clothes didn't fit and left him looking more like a child in his father's hand-downs, but in truth he was glad to be rid of his uniform.

They had put him in the servants' quarters at the top of the house. He had at his disposal a whole suite of rooms which led off from a central passage. The door at the head of the stairs was kept locked but he was free to wander, like a ghost, all the rooms on the floor. It was evident the small musty apartments had not been used in a decade. They were cluttered with all sorts of lumber; dusty boxes, a broken toy pram, frames of bedsteads. The toy pram interested him; it was evidence of children having lived here at some time. He felt, correctly, that it must have been before Slattery's time. Some blankets tossed in a corner were all his bedding. The silent Factor paid him a further visit to leave three volumes bearing the title *Burke's Bestiary*. Upon inspection he found them to contain coloured illustrations of animals and birds with long, hard names he could not read.

Most of the rooms were lit by skylights but at one side of the house was a window. It looked between the columns of a classical balustrade, over the lawns, and down to the white-capped sea. Jacob Slattery enjoyed fine sea views. If he cared to, he could pick out his vessels in the harbour from his morning-room and watch them put to sea as he ate breakfast.

Now the harbour was thickly clustered with vessels waiting for the seas to abate. The sea lay blank and grey, touched here and there with flecks of white. The wind hummed about the roof of the big house making the boy imagine his high perch was a ship's crow's-nest.

Despite *Burke's Bestiary* he was left with his thoughts for company most of the time. The horror of last night, when he realised who his new master was to be, had receded a little, though it lurked there in his mind continually. Part of him wanted to believe that this was coincidence, that Slattery had no notion he had been seen yesterday. Even so, another insistent murmur told him this was no chance happening – why else was he kept locked up with nothing to do?

He kept his face to the glass and watched the gulls as they strove to ride the wind. The sea was blank, no ship moved in or out of the harbour. He felt very alone. Even in McMurdo's there had been friends, companions in misery. He had found time to set a few snares and sell the odd rabbit. He had chafed because he was not free to go out when he wanted to. He had yearned after ferrets and dogs of his own and the liberty of the fields at dawn.

What would he say when Slattery came? Nothing. No good ever came of telling.

But there returned the memory of Slattery's face as he gazed down at him the previous evening.

'He knows,' he said aloud, 'them eyes looking down into me. He knows I saw him.'

He rubbed at the grime of the window making a porthole through which he could see the world more clearly. He must be sixty feet up at least. The cold of a dead room was gnawing at his vitals but what was worse than that was the thick dread which came whenever he thought of his new master.

'Run away.' He spoke aloud for company; his voice was his only companion, 'Before he kills me too.'

Brave words. Factor left the door ajar when he came in; if he could make a dash for it, catch his jailor unawares, perhaps there was hope.

'Perhaps,' he said, and breathing on the glass, began to polish it.

A few days later Inspector Trumper called on Mr Slattery at his office.

'Ah, the inner sanctum, the holy of holies.' He glanced about the plainly-furnished room, 'This is where you deal in tonnages and calculate the price of raw cane sugar in Jamaica, or wherever. Very Spartan.'

Slattery was erect, in his shirt sleeves, at a tall desk. 'I believe I mentioned to you before, Inspector, how dull our work is.'

'Indeed, no,' Trumper was in good form, 'think of the romance of those faraway places, Tobago . . . er . . . Cape Horn. Think of all those cargoes bound for Cumberland. Those clerks I passed just now, heads bowed, working away sending off consignments and orders to the ends of the globe! Bye the bye,' he observed, 'they all seemed to be working terribly hard.'

'I run what my merchant-men would call a "tight ship".' replied Slattery drily. 'What can I do for you, Inspector?'

'Not a thing – No, I was passing and thought a friendly call would not be amiss. I meet so few men of your calibre in my trade. I thought you delivered your evidence so well yesterday – clear voice, firm tone, most impressive. Are you still poorly?'

'I beg your pardon?'

'Are you still unwell? You looked peaky yesterday and even more washed-out today. My dear fellow, you should sleep more – at least ten hours is my golden rule. Do you have a nightcap? Don't forget the brandy in warm milk, just a scrape of nutmeg. My wife prepares it for me with her own dear hands. I expect your man could do it for you.'

As he spoke Trumper walked about the office, opening a ledger here, blowing the dust off a volume there. 'Murder by person or persons unknown. Well, I expect we'll make an arrest soon.'

'You do?' Slattery kept his tone polite, inwardly damning Trumper for an interfering fool.

'Oh yes, we have your description – he can't have got far on foot. Very helpful you were there Mr Slattery. I thought it only proper of the coroner publicly to thank you for giving up your valuable time to attend. Nice touch, I thought, showed a proper sense of priorities. After all, it is you merchants and manufacturers who make this nation of ours so great. Oh yes, we'll catch the rogue sure enough. You see, we have one invaluable weapon in our armoury.'

'What could that be?'

'Time, my dear fellow, time. We can go home and eat our muffin for tea with a clear conscience.' Trumper glanced surreptitiously to see what effect he was having. 'But our man can't. Murder most foul will worm inside him and destroy his appetite and his rest. I've seen it happen before. It won't give him any peace. It will sit – metaphorically speaking – upon his shoulders like some great black burden until he is driven to cast it off. He'll do something foolish and then –'

Trumper made a sudden snatch at a spider as it descended lazily above the rows of books.

Slattery started and watched with a horrid fascination as Inspector Trumper opened his hand and burst out laughing.

'Damn me if I haven't missed it!'

'What then?' asked Slattery.

'What then? Why he'll be hanged and a good thing too.'

'Inspector –'

Trumper paused in the doorway.

'If you sent a man to the gallows could you still go home to your muffin for tea?'

Trumper stared at him. 'My dear fellow, I don't make the laws.'.

Slattery was lost in thought. 'No – society must have its price, I suppose. We all must die, hanging at least has the virtue of being a sure and speedy end.' He shuddered. 'What is worse is the display. The eyes –'

'Of the common herd? Sitting in the dock for all to see and wonder at? Yes, to men of our susceptibilities that would be hard. But we are dealing with an habitual criminal here. He would be used to it all.'

Slattery picked up his pen again. 'Of course. Good day, Inspector.'

Redemption stirred as the key turned in the door and candlelight flared into the room. He slept on the pile of bedding in the corner.

'Ah, here you are.'

Slattery had come. A different Slattery to the one he remembered, the once smooth hair was tangled, the skin of his cheeks hung in folds. He seemed at once fleshier and thinner. He was like a drunken man, fumbling, uncertain.

'Let me see you.' He held the light over the boy. 'So young ... what time is it? No matter ... night time, night time. I want to ask you a question. I won't harm you.' He sank to his knees. 'Tell me the truth for I know if you lie. Do you understand?'

The boy nodded.

'Good. The question is this.' Slattery paused. 'Did I do that thing? You know the deed I mean. Did I do it?'

He swayed and sighed. 'I know it. I see it in your face. Why do I think sometimes that I am dreaming?' He looked oddly at the boy. 'Why do I still see him – what is your name?'

Redemption told him.

'Redemption.' He gave a cracked laugh. 'Redemption. Tell me, Redemption why do I still see Sol Rim? Don't shrink away. I will not hurt you. Your life is safe with me. I want you to understand that – there will be no more blood.' Slattery raised his hand and brought it into the light; he seemed to examine his fingers, turning them over and over in the yellow glare while the candle threw the huge shadow of his hand onto the wall. 'So much blood,' he said. 'But there will be no more of it. I am a respectable man ... respected. They respect me – they thanked me in court for giving up my time.' He switched his gaze to Redemption with an abruptness that made the boy start. 'You are the only person in the world who stands between me and madness. You belong to me. You have been bought and sold. Do you understand what I am saying? You are the only person I can speak with about that ... *thing* I did. There

is no one else . . . I own you. Do you know . . .'

The candle flared and his eyes gleamed. 'I haven't slept since it happened? I drag my couch from room to room, Factor thinks I am quite mad already. Often I think of you up here but I have kept away until tonight. Every time I try to sleep it all begins again in my head. Now Trumper has started to pester me. Trumper has begun to suspect something. Am I a bad man?'

There was no need to answer this abrupt question. Slattery continued in an urgent whisper. 'Soon I will be lost. It is all part of the contract – there's a price to be paid, you see. I tell you I saw *him* tonight, standing in the corner of the room grinning at me. Blighted be the day we met! What's that?' He cast a terrified glance at the door as the handle rattled and turned.

It was Factor, fully dressed, bearing a lamp.

He glanced quickly from Slattery to the boy. 'I heard talking.'

'We have not met before . . . Redemption and I.' Slattery's shadow appeared immense as he stood up.

'It is a funny time to come calling, I'm thinking,' said Factor, bluntly.

'I do not keep you to think,' responded Slattery, sharply.

'No, master.'

'How long will you keep me here?' Redemption's voice, pitched barely above a whisper, shifted their attention to where he crouched against the wall.

Factor looked to Slattery for a reply. Slattery blew out his candle.

'Light me down, Factor.'

At the doorway he paused. 'I mean you no harm,' he said. 'Believe me, I mean you no harm.'

The footsteps clattered until they reached the carpeted level below where they died away.

'Lord help us, he's a madman,' whispered Redemption. 'I'm lost altogether – saw him did he?' He drew his blankets closer about his ears. 'Well, he saw a ghost, nowt else. And he knows I was there – I never telt but he looked right into me. I must be gormless to land up here – why he'll never let me go!'

The truth of it dawned slowly.

'Aye, what a house this is. Mad Slattery and that Factor that never says a word. And me up here till I'm a skellington.'

If there were tears on his pillow his head teemed with ideas for escape.

'Jesus bright, Jesus bright, keep us safe this very night.'

With this muttered prayer he closed his eyes and attempted sleep.

'Slattery had a wife?' Inspector Trumper threw the last of the crumbs from his office window and stared at the pigeons, 'You told me he couldn't "bear" women.'

'He's known for it. But it says here he had a wife.'

'Sergeant, are your sources sound?'

'The Metropolitan Police,' said the sergeant heavily. 'Very prompt *and* efficient.'

'Very well, carry on – hello, here come the starlings, now we'll see some fun.'

'Sir –'

'Yes, sergeant, I apologise, you were saying . . .'

'You haven't heard the choicest part – she was murdered.'

'Well, well. Murder again.' Inspector Trumper sat down. 'How unfortunate. So he came to Cumberland a wealthy man – whose money was it?'

'Hers.'

'You don't say so. Alibi?'

'Yes. He was at a dinner, there are two hundred guests to swear to it.'

'Two hundred guests and he didn't take his wife. Now there's a man who was master in his own house. I have to take my wife and daughters.'

' "Ornaments to Wellshead society" the paper calls 'em,' said the sergeant with a grin. 'The house was broken into that evening. Considerable number of items taken, plate and jewelry. They even had the rings from her fingers. It is thought that she disturbed the intruders.'

'And did they ever catch these murderous felons?'

'No – no one was ever taken.'

'What do you say to my notions about Jacob Slattery now. sergeant?'

The sergeant frowned. 'I'm not a clever man, sir. These guesses aren't in my line, but I grant you that you could have something here. Only could have, mind you – it's a very bad thing to make assumptions in matters of this nature.'

Inspector Trumper did his best to appear humble. 'How true. There's the voice of the seasoned hand for you.'

He polished the surface of his desk with his cuff. 'I'll tell you the truth, sergeant, I want to get the whole affair settled one way or another by Christmas. Christmas is the time to be at home in jollity but I know this wretched thing will cloud my brow and spoil my appetite. My daughters will shun me, my wife reproach me, and life will be unendurable.' He shrugged, 'I may look the fool yet. Someone will pick up Slattery's bearded tramp and there will be an end to it.'

'You don't believe that.'

'If he walked in here now and gave himself up I shouldn't believe in him. The bearded tramp is a creature of ectoplasm, I can put my fingers through him, he doesn't exist. Why did no one else see him?'

He returned to the window. 'There. Not a pigeon in sight. The starlings have won the day.' He sighed. 'Ours is a vile trade.'

'It's been good to me.'

'Yes, stable employment, free uniform, police house, pension. Respect – I'm sure your neighbours respect you, sergeant. What sort of child were you at school? Were you a monitor or a prefect? I certainly wasn't – I was an idle and ill-mannered oaf, lucky to escape without a sacking. Like most of my class I was brought up to be above the law in many respects. I only chose this profession to annoy my father. Now I discover I've become a sort of moral prefect free to poke my nose wherever

I will. The trouble is that sometimes the stench is rather overwhelming.'

The sergeant nodded sagely, he had only the haziest of notions of what his superior was talking about but he liked him and felt sympathetic. 'You're too feeling for this job, sir,' he said.

'Ah,' Inspector Trumper lit a cigar. 'That's what it is, indeed that's what it is. Still, the scales of Justice must be balanced. The sword of whatsisname will come crashing down.'

When there was enough light to see, Redemption began his search for a suitable weapon. By the light of day it seemed a foolhardy notion to attempt escape but the alternative was to spend the rest of his days locked up with mad Slattery.

The lumber was discouraging; boxes, a fender - too big - pieces of crockery, a washstand or two. He broke up a picture frame but the result was too small and light to be of much use in striking a blow. His plan was to wait until Factor came with his food and strike him a disabling blow on the hand or arm and then dart out of the open door. Simple, he thought pessimistically, about as much chance as a fly at a bull.

Across the curtainless window was a dilapidated curtain pole. With one end screwed off, it made the perfect weapon. He set about his mattress with it and raised such a dust that he was seized with a fit of sneezing. He hid the pole between the mattress and the wall. Now, he felt, he was ready.

But Factor did not come. The day lengthened emptily and the only sounds he heard were caused by the wind or the mice. He was forgotten, it seemed. Before now Factor had come regularly during the day with his meals. Although his original taciturnity had not quite disappeared he seemed to look upon him with a kindlier eye, urging him to 'eat up' or 'git thy meat'. By his speech Redemption guessed he was a countryman from the farms and villages inland. His resolve to disable him with a well-aimed blow alternately flared or weakened. As it grew dark he grew weary and fell asleep.

'Here, git thy meat, lad.'

Factor was shaking him.

'Did thoo think thoo was forgot?'

How could he do it now? He had planned to lie in wait by the door, not to be caught asleep.

'I've fetched thee another book. Drink thy milk.' Factor offered him a small volume. '*Robinson Crusoe*. 'Tis about someone like thee.'

Redemption flung it away in disgust. 'Was he locked away with a madman – and a man that says nowt?' He felt cold and drank the warm milk greedily.

'Mr Slattery is not mad. Nay, Robinson Crusoe was cast up on a desert island with no friend.' Factor glanced about, 'This is thy desert island, but not for much longer. Mr Slattery has found an opening for thee. Thoo'll be leaving us shortly.'

Redemption did not know whether to be pleased or dismayed.

'What's ganna be done with me?'

'Never thee mind. I've said nowt.'

With this Factor relapsed into his accustomed silence. There were rooms full of books in this house and Factor was the only one to read them. Had Redemption been staying longer it was possible that under the servant's guidance his education would have improved.

At McMurdo's there were great happenings. Mrs Biggs was leaving. It was understood that an unexpected legacy enabled her to give up her post. She was going somewhere great to live, Manchester had been hinted at although another rumour favoured Liverpool. At any rate she was taking the train this morning and her baggage was to follow. Everyone was pleased; the staff of the orphanage never liked her, the children never liked her, the chairman of governors always felt uneasy in her presence. It was a relief she was going but everyone, apart from the children, pretended it was not. The chairman said what an exemplary influence she had been; he said that her joy was their sorrow, as they would be losing a paragon. The children applauded his words; a paragon sounded like a species of dragon. Certainly no one seemed sorrowful, cheerful would have been a better description. The chairman presented her with a sampler which someone had found somewhere, 'Strength and Honour are her Clothing', it said.

For her part, Mrs Biggs did not pretend. She returned the assembled gaze of McMurdo's with a glance that said plainly they were so much dirt beneath her feet. She barely acknowledged the sampler but said, with a curl of her lip, that she hoped the standards of cleanliness at McMurdo's would not again lapse to what they had been before her arrival.

She swept out leaving the startled chairman the task of dismissing the assembly. Everyone sighed with relief.

Down at the harbour there was a bustle of activity. The wind had abated and vessels prepared to leave Wellshead; there was a concerted yawning and stretching among the sailors. Old salts shook their heads and said the dirty weather was by no means over, but younger men mocked them. There was an eagerness to be away, a great deal of whistling and singing on deck.

Among the vessels that took an early opportunity to leave was the *Lord Henry*, a grimy collier which ran coals for Slattery to Ireland. As far as anyone knew, she carried no cargo but there was nothing untoward in that.

FIVE

He was in a rowing boat with Mrs Biggs. The boat rocked and the oars creaked as she bent to her task. 'A bold boy,' she crooned. Was he bald? Then Slattery was kneeling by the bed rocking back and forth his knees creaking like the oars, 'Redemption, Redemption . . .'

When he woke up the rocking motion did not stop. He lay quietly listening to strange sounds as waves slapped and crashed against the hull, ropes creaked in the block, canvas flapped. There was a strong smell of tar and coal dust. Feet passed over his head with a hollow, drumming noise. His side hurt where he had slept on a hard, squarish object in his pocket. It was *Robinson Crusoe*. He sat up and narrowly missed banging his head. As he did so the cabin door opened and in stepped a seaman wearing a striped night-cap and a greasy apron.

'I thought you would never wake.'

The seaman regarded him with a friendly grin. There was something engaging about his appearance. Although his face was pitted with pock marks he looked no more than twenty-four. His hair fell to his shoulders in a mass of fair, unruly curls; when he smiled there was a gap between his teeth. He sported an ear-ring in one ear and his arms were covered in tattoos.

'I'm Cropper,' he said.

It was the first friendly face Redemption had seen in a long time. He liked him, noting his careless attitude as he stood, easily riding the motion of the waves.

'I'm at sea,' he observed, stupidly.

'Aboard the *Lord Henry*, God help us. The master is still

drunk and the mate – Spavin – would like my guts for breakfast. Eat?' He glanced at the greasy mess in the bowl. 'Fish-head soup? There's no knowing what goes on in that galley. No? Can't say as I blame you.' He tossed it out of the porthole. 'I expect they'll throw it back directly,' he said.

Redemption laughed in spite of himself. He winced too at the aching of his head.

'You've had a Mickey Finn,' went on Cropper. 'They brought you on board last night dead to the world. It was only by chance that I happened to be there – the rest of the crew was entertaining themselves at The Blue Anchor. Wasn't Spavin wild? The gent that brought you said you was a poor traveller and needed sedation. Leastways that's what I thought he muttered, I can never understand the way of speaking up here. Seeing as I *was* there Spavin has put me in charge of you and says he'll have my liver if I blab. Blab what?' Cropper's grin showed the gap between his teeth. 'I only shipped on this jolly-boat to run away from a woman what wanted to marry me –'

'What are they ganna do with me?' Redemption cut across the flow of words. As he had been speaking Cropper had peered out of the port-hole, glanced under the cot, and finally sat down next to the boy.'

'Are they ganna kill me?'

Cropper was startled.

'Where's Slattery?' His dream was still fresh in his mind.

'Easy boy, you sit back there. There ain't no Slattery on this ship, don't worrit yourself. There's Tully, he's the master, and Spavin – may his nose rot off – but no Slattery.'

'What are they ganna do with me?' repeated Redemption.

'Blest if I know. But they ain't a going to kill you.' Cropper's voice was concerned. 'Why, I wouldn't let 'em. I wouldn't let anyone do that. We ain't pirates you know.'

'Thou can't do owt. No one can help me.' said Redemption, bleakly.

Cropper's quick sympathies were engaged. It was plain there was more to this business than met the eye. He wished he could cheer the pale, spiky-haired boy.

'Look here,' he said. 'When I was your age I was tramping the streets of London with a tray selling ribbons. When I wasn't doing that I was in the brickfields trapping finches to sell. When I wasn't doing that . . . I made out. I'm still here ain't I?'

'They're all agin me. All of 'em.'

'I ain't agin you.' Cropper watched as the boy kept his face to the wall. 'I like you – I do. Things don't ever get so bad without they get better. Every cloud,' he said sententiously, 'has a silver lining. I expect I'm it. I like the look of you. You look like you can take care of yourself, you do. You won't give up – not you.'

'But what's to become of me?' persisted Redemption.

Cropper sighed. 'I'm only Cropper. No one tells me anything. But I'll tell you what I'll do – if you promise to cheer yourself up – I'll find out for you. That's what I'll do.' He had nothing to lose. He had only joined the ship on its previous trip out of Liverpool and already the antagonism between himself and the mate Spavin, the effectual ruler of the ship, was at breaking-point. Although a young man, Cropper had knocked about the world a great deal. He was wise to its ways while still retaining his original simplicity of character. He could not abide to see injustice or unfairness. He was the only man in a mean-spirited ship who dared stand up to Spavin. Now, it seemed, they were involved in some dirty business with this boy. He had been lounging on deck – thinking of the girl he had run away from in Liverpool – when the small figure had been bundled aboard. It was close to midnight and everyone was at carouse. Everyone, it seemed, except himself and Spavin. Spavin had appointed him, with many an oath and injunction to secrecy, to be the boy's keeper and the two of them had carried him down to the cabin. Cropper thought it odd then that the boy had not a scrap of kit with him, no bag of any kind. The thick-tongued countryman who brought him stayed only long enough to see it done before driving the carriage away from the deserted quay.

Direct questioning of Spavin was out of the question, Cropper decided. The thing to do was to avoid any clash with the mate and to try to catch any hint, or word, that may fall from him or Mr Tully. Meantime he could make the boy's voyage as pleasant as possible.

'Come along, young trouble.' He said that evening, pleased to see that some colour had returned and that some spirit still lurked in the boy's eyes. 'We shall give you an airing. Spavin wants you kept fresh.'

On the fo'c'sle no-one was about, it was dark although lanterns shed dim pools of light at intervals. Cropper leant over the side and spat, watching the white of the ship's wake as it glinted in the dark.

'There's Wales.' To port Redemption could make out a darker smear within the dark and then, here and there, the glimmer of lights. Wales. He felt something stir in his blood, he was travelling, this was his first experience of an outside world and it was thrilling, regardless of circumstances. In a respectful way he hinted that Cropper must have seen a lot of the world.

'I've seen a lot of everything,' agreed Cropper. 'I've had to look after myself as long as I can remember.'

'Didn't no one help you?'

'Aye – lots of folk give me a kind word and a shilling here and there. There was Father Mulvanny now, he would never let a chap starve. But mainly I found my own shelter and put food in my own belly. Once you learn to do that there ain't a great deal to be afeard of.'

Redemption thought of this in silence for some time. The freshening breeze whipped about them and his lungs filled with good sea air.

'Thou doesn't like Spavin,' he remarked.

Cropper had contrived to light a short, very black pipe, but he removed it from his mouth for this.

'Spavin,' he returned, feelingly, 'is a snake. The only person who stands up to him on this ship is me. He thinks he's got me where he wants me but I lay I'll surprise him yet.'

'Isn't thou afraid of him?' asked Redemption curiously.

'I ain't afeard of no-one.' Cropper puffed at his pipe for a time, then removed it again. 'Did I mention Father Mulvanny? He once said something to me, he said, "The shadow is always bigger than the cross, Cropper." I never understood that but when he explained it I think I do. He meant that if you think about a thing you get afeard. If you face up to it the fear goes away. It's the same with Spavin. All this lot,' he jerked his thumb at the deck. 'They walk in terror of him, frightened of his shadow. Me, I stand up to him, he ain't nothing but a fat old man with an evil look in his eye.'

Redemption moved closer to him under the lee of the rail and they remained in companionable silence until the pipe was smoked out. Cropper knocked it out and sent a stream of sparks to windward.

'We shall come up regularly,' he promised. 'I shall look after you on this ship.'

Redemption slept easier that night than he had a right to. The first he knew of morning was of being pitched headlong onto the floor. The *Lord Henry* was rolling horribly. Even though it was still dark he could make out snow, pale and wet, on the port-hole. The wind was up again, flapping the canvas like gunshot, humming through the rigging. The whole ship felt as if it was being stretched and pulled taut. Winter, who had slept for the space of only one day, was awake and angry. As the day lengthened it grew not brighter but remained a dim, brooding grey. Conditions worsened.

When Cropper opened the cabin-door he all but fell in. There was snow on his shaggy hair and his oilskins were slicked with wet.

'Hullo,' as he steadied himself he glanced up at the roof of the cabin where water dripped. 'That's bad. The seas are getting worse and no mistake. We come over 'em and through 'em and sometimes I wonder what we'll see on the other side – the pit I shouldn't think. Hullo, young friend you do look green. Here – 'tis only bread and coffee but you must line your belly on a day like this.' He slopped it down and blew on his hands. 'Snow at sea, you'd think we was in Russian waters.'

He sat down heavily next to Redemption who cupped the lukewarm drink with care. Cropper was excited, there was a wild sparkle in his eye as he glanced at the boy.

'I've tumbled 'em,' he said. 'I know what's up.'

He stopped Redemption's exclamation. 'There ain't much time. They need all hands at the moment if this tub is to remain afloat, but this is it. I catched Spavin and Tully worrying whether they could seek shelter and still make their rendezvous. We're bound for the port of London where they have instructions to put you aboard a vessel bound for Australia. Australia!'

His breath showed like smoke. 'You may well look at me like that! You'll be travelling steerage and if you survive the voyage it'll only be to become bound over to some skinflint farmer who'll work you to death inside three months.'

'Slattery wants shut of me,' said Redemption huskily. So that was it.

The wild light played in Cropper's eye as he smiled.

'And do you want to be pushed out of the way? Do you? Of course you don't. I been thinking. I'm leaving this ship first time we touch land. I'm off and I'll help you jump ship with me. Plenty have done it. Come with me.'

Redemption nodded dumbly.

'I knew you would.' Cropper beat his fist on his thigh. 'Won't it put Spavin's nose out of joint though? All his villainy shall come a cropper because of Cropper! Here, I don't even know your name.'

The boy told him.

'That's a curious name. Your father weren't a preacher by any chance?'

Redemption informed him briefly that he had no notion of his father's occupation, nor his mother's for that matter.

'Well Red – I shall call you Red, t'other's too churchy – that's a shame. When you was low yesterday I had no idea the way matters stood. My own mother died when I was a good deal younger than you are now. God Bless her.' He crossed himself. 'Killed by a tinker woman who flung a pot at her head. We was put on the streets because of it, the only one to help us was the priest. He set me up with my first tray of ribbons –'

There was a muffled shout of command from above and dimly, above the ever-increasing roar, the sound of hurrying feet. Cropper had to raise his voice, although he was almost hoarse from previous efforts.

'We'll have to ride it out somewhere or I miss my guess. We're shipping too much water. They're taking in sail and will put men on the pumps if this goes on for much longer. Spavin will be looking for me.'

'Will we have to fight 'em?'

Cropper was delighted. 'No, Red, though I truly think you would. We must fox 'em with guile. It'll be all I can do not to bust out laughing in Spavin's face.'

The blizzard showed no sign of relenting. To the other sounds of the storm was added the clanking of the ship's pumps. So steep were the seas on either hand that the troughs between the waves were like valleys and the little collier was dwarfed. The waters heaved with awe-inspiring power. The sailors on the *Lord Henry*, snow in their eyes and beards, attached themselves by lines to their ship and worked doggedly, knowing that without this precaution one slip meant sure death. Talk was become impossible in the gale but the glances passed between man and man were eloquent enough. This would be a close-run thing.

Alone in the dark cabin Redemption clung to his bunk and fought to keep nausea at bay. The lurches the ship gave were fearful enough but what was worse was the mighty crash of the waves against her. To the boy they hinted at forces and powers beyond his imaginings. For all that he was in good spirits. If they all died there was no helping it. If they did not Cropper was with him and Cropper was a match for anyone. Cropper was afraid of nothing.

The master of the *Lord Henry* knew the waters he was plying. As afternoon turned into evening the battered ship sought refuge along the coast, dropping anchor to ride out the storm in the lee of the mighty headland which upreared through the gloom. The clanking of the pumps continued long after they had come to rest. The snow had stopped but there were drifts of it in the scuppers, the rigging was covered, the capstan had been turned into a squat snowman. By the lamps which burned on deck the ship presented a frozen, lonely sight. The seas ran with less violence in the lee but the shadowy figures of the crew continued work until the master was satisfied. The men went below in twos and threes, most of them had not eaten or had any drink all day, at the last a period of calm settled on the tired ship.

Some time later Cropper opened Redemption's door.

'They're passing the rum bottle - I volunteered to take the watch. Would you like an airing? I had rather been on deck today than down here, Red. Steady as you go, 'tis precious slippery. My hands are flayed like two slabs of butcher's meat - we've had some work this day.'

He led the way up the ladder. Everything was rimed with ice and snow and the bitter cold made Redemption gasp. On deck all was quiet although an occasional snatch of song was carried from below.

'Like pigs at a trough,' muttered Cropper. 'Sailing men will take their liquor - there's nothing can be done to prevent it. Wait.'

He disappeared into the gloom. While he was gone Redemption strained his eyes to the nearby coast. What little he could make out was that they were near, very near, two hundred yards or less, before the shore began. He hugged himself to keep warm. The wind was so keen it made his bones ache. There was nowhere to shelter, everything was covered in ice or snow.

When Cropper came back he was grinning.

'Are you still game, young Red?'

'Aye,' whispered Redemption, his gaze still on the land.

'I see you are. Then let us take our chance - did you hear aught just now?'

'When? No, I heard nowt - the wind.'

'Then no one else will have heard. Come and look.'

Bobbing in the darkness below was the ship's boat which Cropper had lowered secretly.

'No time like the present,' Cropper muttered. 'We shan't ever get so favourable a wind. We're not far from the shore and they're all puddled with work and drink. Follow me.' He swung down nimbly and was soon seated. 'No noise!'

The suddenness of his opportunity left no time for thought. The frozen rope burned his hands as he slithered and kicked himself down. The *Lord Henry* lurched and rolled, Cropper had to exert great skill to avoid being swamped as he kept the boat alongside.

'Hurry now, Red!'

Redemption had realised, with a quick fear, that the rope was short and he would have to jump for it. Under such circumstances, at night with both the ship and the boat so lively, even a seasoned hand would have thought it no disgrace to end up in the water. He faltered.

'Look lively, Red! Hurry now!'

Still Redemption clung to the ship's side.

'Damn me! If I won't go without you.' Cropper made a move as if to cast off. He closed his eyes and jumped, sailing for an infinitesimal time through a black void before landing safe with a clatter that winded him. Cropper cast off without a word.

SIX

Now Cropper had served with a whaler and had put down in worse seas than this. Then there had been a full crew to row, now he was unaided. It was a perilous thing but he made light of it, pulling steadily for the shore and cajoling his boat along with tender words. He was aware they might strike hidden rocks or be swamped by the racing seas yet his untroubled brow gave no hint of it. He grinned at the boy. He knew it was a hard thing to leap into a moving boat at night, he knew also that if either of them landed in the water they would most likely freeze to death. He was a lucky man and knew that chances were to be taken, so he grinned. They did not splinter or overturn, before many moments had passed he brought them ashore with a rush. He beached the boat, cursing softly at the coldness of the water about his ankles. They both glanced wordlessly at the lights of the *Lord Henry* as she rode at anchor.

The path from the beach was a steep gully and the snow lay inches deep in places, in others it had drifted even deeper. It was a stumbling scramble they had out of that place, toiling upwards, the only moving creatures in a still landscape. At the top they paused to catch their breath.

'We must find shelter,' said Cropper. 'We can't spend the night out of doors.'

Already their feet and finger ends were numb with cold.

'My watch ends in two hours. We must put a distance between us and them before we rest.'

In parts, where the snow was not so deep, they were able to run. They had to struggle through the drifts, Cropper beating down the snow to help the boy. The thought of pursuit was always there; whenever they paused they strained to hear the noises that would tell them the game was afoot. Posts, bushes, stunted trees took on new and sinister guises in the night.

'You there!' said Cropper, to a hunchback figure along their path.

'I knowed it was a stump all the time,' he said, when it proved to be the ruin of an old hawthorn with snow drifted about it. 'Come along now. Don't dawdle.'

How long they ran for Redemption didn't know. His heart was pounding and he had a painful stitch in his side. Cropper seemed unaffected, but as the hours wore away he glanced more and more at his young companion. They had reached a kind of moor. Their path was protected by a line of stunted hedges but it was plain that the snow was much thicker here. There was no more running, just a high-kneed walk which was even more tiring. Out of the dark loomed the shape of some low dwelling. They listened.

'No dogs?' asked Cropper.

Redemption shook his head.

'Who would live out here without dogs?' Cropper did not wait for an answer but plunged through the snow to the cottage, for such they could now see it was. Cropper called the boy over saying the place was deserted.

It was a miserable dwelling divided into two apartments. One had evidently been for the cottager and the other for his animals. Such was the isolation of its position that it had been abandoned. Not entirely though, there was a neat pile of fencing stacked by the manger and straw in the corner. Cropper struck a match, noting the rotten harness hanging by a nail, the sacking at the window. He kicked the manger.

'We need fuel. That will burn.'

There was a hearth in the living-quarters. In the chimney corner he found the greasy stub of a candle which he lit. The room was bare save for one rickety chair by the fire, the position in which it had seen service for so many years.

'Sit on the straw, Red.'

Redemption did so without a word, lying back and closing

his eyes. His heart beat his chest like a club and he trembled with exhaustion. When he awoke he had been moved near the fire, Cropper had piled up dry straw for him and carried him through. The chair was burning and crackling furiously. He coughed.

'Chimney ain't been swept,' observed Cropper tersely. He was peeling a large turnip with his clasp knife. 'There's a path from the back of here to some woodland. It's allus wise to know where you stand. Drink some of that.'

He reached out a flat bottle from his sailor's pea-jacket and uncorked it with his teeth.

It was like fire. Tears started in his eyes and he was seized with another fit of coughing. As it burned down his throat he became conscious of a delicious warmth spreading through his limbs. Cropper tossed over an oilskin wallet full of ship's biscuit and began to roast the turnip by the fire. He had found time to steal the biscuit earlier that day.

After they had eaten Cropper lit his pipe and stared at the flames. He seemed dissatisfied with his pipe and put it away after a while.

'Time was,' he muttered, 'baccy meant more to me than vittles or women. Especially women . . .' He sighed hopelessly. In an attempt to rouse himself he turned to Redemption.

'I say, Red,' he exclaimed. 'I don't wish to put my nose where it ain't wanted but do you think you could give me a hint as to what all this is about? We haven't exactly had time before but there's a long night ahead and no one to disturb us.'

Redemption told him the full story. While he spoke Cropper listened intently with a frown. His eyes brooded as the murder was described, flashed at Mrs Biggs' treachery, grew thoughtful at the mention of Slattery again, and finally lit with triumph as he realised the full part he had played in the drama.

'Why, it's like a story book!' he said. 'I helped to do the lot of 'em. Me, Cropper, the one everybody said would never amount to much. They said I should never learn to settle down but at least I've done some good. I'll tell you what, Red my boy, we must finish the job we've begun this night.'

He lit his pipe again and began to smoke it with enjoyment. 'That Slattery must be brought to book and I'm the lad to help do it.'

If his sympathies had been with Redemption before he was as now completely committed to him as if the injuries had been done to himself.

'Why, he's a rich man. 'Tis only your word against his, you know.'

Redemption knew it.

'A man like that can buy and sell his way out of any amount of trouble. The world ain't a fair place, nor a just one, nor a kind one.' He ruminated further. 'The world's a terrible place for gammon – "With a Rowley Powley gammon and spinach".' He sang this last part in a thoughtful undertone.

'Putney,' he said, at last. 'That's what the man – Sol Rim – said was it?'

'Aye, "Putney in the county of Surrey". He –' Redemption had noticed it at once. 'He talked like thee.'

'London – Sol Rim was from London. That's a fair guess I'd say. Half the wrong 'uns in the world live there. When you think about it this is a London story – Putney ain't far up the river.'

'Thou never met him?'

'Who – Sol Rim?' Cropper laughed. 'No, I never did. London ain't a poky little town you know. Why, I expect I don't know half the folk as lives there.' He laughed again at Redemption's disappointment.

'Mind you – Putney is the place to make for. I'll tell you why – some of the dead woman's folk might just be interested in our tale. Ten year ain't such a long time. London is grand and big, you'll like it.'

With this promise Cropper knocked out his pipe and laid it by.

'Now we'll turn in. I am dead beat from the day and we have a tramping life ahead of us. We're safe enough here.'

He put his cap across his eyes and was soon snoring. He had forgotten all about the girl in Liverpool and the people who said he would never settle down. Not for a moment had he regretted the impulsive way he had befriended the boy and engineered his escape.

Redemption watched the light of the fire flicker on the walls, warm and drowsy. He could see a place where something had once hung and the lighter patch it had left behind, a cheap-looking glass or a picture, perhaps. In his mind he thought of the long dormitory in McMurdo's and a fairy story he had once heard. Something to do with an evil witch who granted a woman a wish. The woman asked for money and next day her baby was run down by the lord's carriage, who tossed her a gold coin for the injury. He had always wished to be away from McMurdo's. Like the woman in the story he had got his wish but someone had died. They would kill him too, if they caught him. He stirred and looked over to where Cropper was sleeping, his curly hair falling back on the earthen floor. Even in repose his face was strong. He had Cropper ... he would be all right. Everything would be all right.

It was morning and Cropper was at the window. The air in the cottage was cold, still tinged with woodsmoke. Sleep had refreshed Redemption and he lazily turned to speak to his friend. Something in Cropper's attitude warned him to silence. He crept to the window, noticing the stout stick Cropper had leant against the wall near him.

'It's Spavin,' said Cropper softly. 'He's rousted them out afore first light. Rot him.'

'What we ganna do?'

'They know we're in here. Our footsteps lead to the door as plain as if we'd left a message saying where we was. What a fool I am!' His tone was bitter. 'Why couldn't it snow some more?'

The group of seamen were in a knot some fifty yards away. Spavin, a squat, balding man with fleshy features was gesticulating in their direction.

'Sam Mossop, Henry Pye, Tommy Kane and young Locke,' muttered Cropper. 'Not an honest man among 'em.'

Last night's carouse had left them fit only for mischief. They stared at the cottage through bloodshot eyes, tightening their grips on the staves they carried, raising them in readiness.

'If they catch us it's all up with you, Red.'

The boy kept his eyes on the men, who stirred restlessly.

'Pick up those matches and my knife and stow 'em in your pockets. Good. Take care of the knife he's a good 'un. I want you to make a run for it now – out of the back window down the path and into the trees I told you about. If I don't come directly don't worry – cut along without me.'

Redemption nodded again. Cropper grinned down at him.

'It ain't the end of the world, Red. Look lively now. I want you to go on the tramp. Head for London and once you get there make for Covent Garden.'

Redemption swallowed hard.

'I'll be on the road somewheres behind you, never fear. Once in Covent Garden find a public house named The Black Cat. I'm known there. We'll meet up there. You can do it, can't you?'

'Aye.' In a whisper.

'Don't forget now – The Black Cat.'

The group of men had strung themselves out in a ragged line and begun their approach.

'Cropper! Is it you in there?' Spavin's voice wheezed and whistled as he spoke.

Cropper replied by coolly breaking the remaining glass of the window with his club, giving himself space. The men stopped.

'That weren't kind, Cropper,' went on Spavin. 'Running away like that. I can hand you over to the law for this. Do you hear me, Cropper?'

He paused to catch his breath.

'Aye,' Cropper's voice was low, serious. The seamen, stock-still, stared back in the direction of his voice, the wind stirring in their hair. Their faces reflected the same hard look Cropper's wore.

'But I won't,' said Spavin, hoarsely. 'Give us the boy and ye may wander where ye will. We allus did rub agin each other the wrong way. I'm glad to be rid of you. Give us the boy, Cropper.' There was menace in his voice and in the baleful look he cast at the cottage.

'I'll see you to the devil first,' replied Cropper, in the same serious tone. 'With your back broke.'

He looked down at the boy. 'Make a run for it, Red. *Now*!'

Redemption took one last look at his friend and then was out of the back window dropping into the snow.

Spavin turned on his men.

'D'ye hear him!'

'Cropper can handle hisself,' volunteered one, Henry Pye.

Spavin's face was black with fury. 'When I finish with him he won't be fit to handle a babby's spoon. I'll spill blood on this snow.'

With this wheezed promise he motioned his men into action.

Acting on a pre-arranged plan two of them went around the back while two more assailed Cropper's window. Spavin was battering at the door. For a while there was a terrific din as fusillades of blows were rained on the woodwork of the old cottage. The two men at Cropper's window, who were neither of them eager to have their heads broken, contented themselves with attempting to break the window frame without thrusting themselves within range of Cropper's club. The structure of the frame, even without glass, prevented them from climbing in. Cropper, who was keeping a tolerably cool head, realised this and turned his attention to the door. The door was stoutly constructed of oak and would have withstood any amount of ill treatment but Cropper could hear that the two men at the back of the house had effected their entry. There was no point in surrendering the initiative. He stationed himself beside the door and opened it. As luck would have it Spavin was at that very moment aiming another huge blow at the wood. He found himself crashing into the room like an angry bull, off balance and in considerable confusion, striking at the empty air. Before he could wheel round, Cropper dealt him a solid crack across the skull, which felled him. The two men from the back, Henry

Pye and Tommy Kane, burst into the room only to stumble over the prone body of their leader. As they milled about, losing their footing, knocking each other over, the final pair, realising that the door was now open, streamed in. The extreme gloom of the room added only to the confusion. Cropper drubbed every head within range while his enemy, befuddled, struck out at random.

'Why Tommy!' cried one. 'Ye've broke my arm.' There followed a volley of the vilest curses. 'Use sense! Where is he? Where's Cropper?'

Cropper dropped his weapon and leapt through the unguarded door taking an opposite direction to Redemption.

'There he goes!'

The four of them followed in full cry leaving Spavin, still not come to his senses, on the earthen floor. Mossop, Pye and Kane all had blood streaming down their faces but they paid it no heed. The pain served only as a goad. Young Locke, one arm hanging uselessly at his side, brought up the rear whooping and yelping like a hound at chase. Cropper ran as speedily as he could, floundering in the deep parts of the snow, leaping ditches, tearing himself through hedges. He intended to divert attention from Redemption for as long as he was able and cared not where he ran. He led the party downhill keeping a good distance from them. He was young and nimble and could run for hours. The moor gave way to more cultivated land and he left the rough track he was following to strike out across the fields, trusting to his luck all the way. He could see the tops of some pines in the distance and had a notion of losing his pursuers among them. Too late, as he reached a crest, did he realise that the woodland belonged to a park and that the park wall ran the length of the field. He was neatly boxed in. He ran on but the wall was too high to be scaled and no friendly bough bent over to help him clamber up. He covered its length finding no opportunity of escape at all. His pursuers hallooed wildly, Locke still barking and yelping like a dog. Cropper was brought to bay and turned to face them.

They were not long in coming up.

'Who's to be the first?' Cropper, unarmed and panting, still had power enough to make them bunch together and halt. They were a cowardly set of men, even when their blood was up.

'I'll entertain you one by one or all together – it's all the same to me. Which of you is man for it?'

In reply young Locke drew back his good arm and let fly at Cropper with a belaying pin from the *Lord Henry*. It struck him on the temple and laid him low at once. As he attempted to rise, spots of blood fell onto the snow. Mossop came forward, a knife open in his hand.

A glance in his eyes showed Cropper his murderous intent.

'What – would you kill me, Mossop?'

As Mossop bent in the act of dispatching Cropper a shot rang out. It took Mossop in the thigh and he let out a shriek as he fell into the snow clutching his leg. Unobserved, another party had followed the crew of the *Lord Henry*.

'This is a pretty business – on my own land too.'

The speaker was a red-faced gentleman dressed for shooting. Behind him quivered two large hunting dogs and with them a servant who held another shotgun at the ready.

'Is this fair play – four against one?'

He strode forward, ignoring the writhing Mossop and spoke to Cropper.

'How are you?'

'Never better,' replied Cropper, and fainted away.

SEVEN

As Slattery, freshly-groomed and pale, set off for his office he was conscious of someone waving to him from across the road. He averted his eyes, pretending he had not seen, but the subterfuge was useless.

'As we are walking in the same direction, mind if I join you?' Inspector Trumper, affable, sidewhiskers newly-brushed, panting.

'I thought you businessmen were abroad earlier than this – it must be nearly eleven.' He fumbled for his timepiece under the folds of his coat. 'Thought so – seven minutes to. Still, you look as though you've been burning the midnight oil. I don't think I ever saw a man as pale as yourself unless he was gracing the mortician's slab at the time, begging your pardon.'

Slattery ignored this and they fell into step. They looked like a pair of gentlemen taking the morning air together. They walked steadily, down the hill past the large and prosperous dwellings of the middle class on either hand. Before them the sea and sky stretched away without colour or feature.

'I loathe this climate,' observed Trumper after an interval. 'The sky presses down so, smothers like a great pillow – don't you think?'

Slattery cleared his throat but did not answer.

'Now the South is different,' went on Trumper, brimful of good humour. 'Did you ever live in the South, Slattery?'

Slattery supposed he had.

'Not Kent, was it?'

It wasn't Kent.

'My dear wife is from Kent – Deal – she adores the sea air

down there . . . Broadstairs, Ramsgate, Deal. She misses it you know. You could say she pines for Deal – ha!' The inspector snorted with laughter. 'Do you know that's rather good in a wooden sort of way – "pines for Deal". I rather think I could work that up into something humorous. Ha! Ha!'

Slattery stopped and stared at him as if he had gone mad. At the same time he angrily rubbed his arm. Trumper had noticed him do the same thing several times already.

'Something the matter?' asked the inspector.

'My skin . . .'

'I say –' Trumper paused. He had the feeling Slattery was on the brink of something. He had never seen him so wrought, so pent-up.

'Not the time of year for fleas. Get your wife – but I forget, you never did marry did you?'

His innocent tone galvanized Slattery. He reared back his head and his gaze was intense enough to awe the policeman. His eyes flicked up and down, regarding Trumper with a violence akin to hatred.

'My skin crawls, Inspector, at your company. Do you have any charge to lay against me?'

'My dear sir –'

'Do you? Or any shred of evidence to connect me with any crime?' He ground his teeth. 'Answer me!'

Trumper tried to suppress the horrid sensation that Slattery had somehow grown in size. 'My dear sir, what can have put such a ridiculous notion –'

'You hang about my house, waylay me in the street, subject me to an unending stream of inane chatter –'

'I say – that's rather strong.'

'I repeat – do you have any charge to lay against me?'

'None. My dear fellow you are rather wild.'

'Then leave me. Do not presume upon my time. Do you think to play cat and mouse with me?' Again a flicker from those implacable eyes. 'Why, you are a joke in this town. Our ways lie separate, do not try to accompany or follow me. Good day.'

Trumper watched Slattery stride away without a word. If he was nettled he did not show it. He lit a cigar and fell into a leisurely meditative amble. He kept to his own thoughts, ignoring the greetings of passersby.

The police station stood in the midst of a busy market town. About its portals played a handful of street urchins who, however often they were shooed away by the impatient sergeant, were irresistibly drawn back by the opportunities afforded of taunting the town drunkards, or on a quiet day, the sergeant himself. By the steps sat an aged flower-seller, no one could remember the time she was not there, no one questioned her right to do so. Inspector Trumper was a particular favourite of hers. Such a gentleman and always buying a flower for his buttonhole or something for his wife.

He was not to be tempted today. 'He thinks to bluff his way out by intimidating me. But Good Lord, what eyes the man has – it was as if Old Nick himself was peeping out at me. I shiver to think of it.'

He tossed the remains of his cigar away and watched the urchins fight over it. He was reminded of the starlings he fed with crumbs each day.

'Poor fellows – I had better throw bread to them than to the birds.' He sighed. 'What a world it is. The wicked prosper while the poor go hungry.'

Jacob Slattery's house was haunted. Not by the ghost of Sol Rim, although Slattery would have taken an oath that he had seen him there in the drawing-room; yes, and smelled his graveyard breath too. But Sol Rim had not appeared again. The figure who haunted the big house was that of the merchant himself.

A great change had come over Slattery in the days since he had murdered Sol Rim. The act had released a flood of guilt and unease. Dark waters lapped about his mind drawing it downward to a madness that horrified him more than any act he had committed.

He thought often of his dead wife. Before she had been shut

out of mind and memory, but the thought that she had been used even as he had used Sol Rim affected him greatly. He remembered the moment when his heavy stick had come down so murderously, splashing the tombstone with blood. It was as if it were her blood.

He slept but little and that uneasily. Each night Factor moved his bed into another room, as if changing his situation would help him sleep. Yet no matter how his brain yearned and his aching limbs cried out for rest, he had only to close his eyes to be taken again to the place he murdered Sol Rim. The alternative was to lie rigid, staring into blackness, scratching at his arms and chest like an animal. When, despite himself, his eyes closed he was once more before the half open gate. It was not day but bright moonlight, bright enough to cast shadows, bright enough to read the words on the stones. The stones were his company and his witnesses. They peopled his dream and watched impassively as he dealt each shuddering blow to the prone figure on the grass. His wife.

He would get up and walk from room to room, touching familiar objects, solid things that were real. His arms and chest irritated him and he scratched angrily. Perhaps it was a dream. The boy Redemption was gone, there was no one that knew. If only Trumper would leave him alone. The frown that gathered his eyebrows grew permanent on his forehead. His skin wasted and became hollow and lined; his eyes were darker, more inward.

His office grew slack. His clerks explained it by muttering to each other that the old man must have had a heavy crash and it was as well to keep your eyes open for another place. He arrived late and left early. He had a habit of breaking off conversation and of staring into space as if everyday matters had become unimportant. The atmosphere of quiet business-like efficiency, which Inspector Trumper had admired so much, was dissipated. The clerks yawned and stretched openly, laughing behind Slattery's back. Their dinners took longer and longer and the afternoon silences were punctuated by snores. The old shop wasn't what it was.

Slattery did not care but fell to musing what he should do. One afternoon his restlessness took him up to the attic where the boy had slept. The bedding was still carelessly tossed in the corner; between the mattress and the wall Slattery found the curtain pole. He weighed it in his hands, it was heavy, as heavy as his stick.

An hour later Factor interrupted his reverie.

'So here ye are!' He was blowing from his long climb up the stairs.

'The boy had a curious name,' remarked Slattery, weighing the stick in his hand, not looking at Factor, 'Redemption.'

'I thought we'd done wi' all this,' muttered Factor glancing about the room.

'If I pay off a promissory note I redeem it,' went on Slattery. 'I buy it back. I wonder what the boy bought back? My life perhaps?'

Factor's glance said plainly that he did not understand his master.

'There was summat bad in all that.'

Slattery flashed a sudden look at him.

'It felt like dirty work, master.'

'You know nothing of dirty work,' replied Slattery softly. That is why I am master and you are man.' He beat gently on the mattress with the stick. 'The boy has gone to Australia to start a new life – where is the dirty work there? You saw him off. He has gone – and taken his secret with him.' He laughed.

'Why have the police been ferreting about the house then? Tell me that.'

'Trumper again!'

'Nay, not Trumper, one of his men. He was talking about burglary, said there'd been some in the vicinity. Tried to invite hisself in.'

'You let him?'

'Nay – no fear of that. I didn't want him poking and prying about the house. I nivver heerd of any burglaries.'

'Trumper!' Slattery's hands were shaking and involuntarily he raised the stick. 'I would he were here now!'

'The policeman brought a message from him – "My guv'nor was particular that your guv'nor should have it", he said, "Tell your guv'nor that some burglars have been known to kill any person left alone in the house. Take care," he said. Silly talk, I call it,' said Factor, contemptuously. 'Just like Trumper to get carried away.'

Slattery seemed to arrive at a sudden resolution. 'I must leave. Ireland's the place.'

'Master?'

'It's Trumper,' said Slattery wildly. 'He won't let me alone. I can't sleep. I'm not myself.'

'A holiday, like?'

'No,' Slattery took control of himself. 'I will leave for good and start anew. I've done it before. I'll sell up and close the house.'

'Just as ye like,' muttered Factor, but his eyes told a different story.

Inspector Trumper, the subject of this conversation, was feeding the birds for the last time. As he tossed out the crumbs he tried hard to repress the wild feeling of excitement he felt at the prospect of his journey. He was elated.

'Holiday?' His sergeant was dumbfounded.

'Leave, Sergeant, official leave. London – heigh ho!'

'But there's the Slattery business –'

'Just so – that's it. The Slattery business is why I'm going. We can't just watch him moon about all the time, that's not police work. No, turn over his past, look for a motive, investigate his old haunts. That's the work for me – if anything happens you can telegraph me – here is the address of the police station I will be operating from. Very central – I have many friends in the Metropolitan Force.' Inspector Trumper tried to say this without condescension.

'I suppose they're all university chaps down there.'

'Sergeant, there is a note of sarcasm in your tone which ill becomes your normal bluff, good-tempered self. As far as I know I am the only university chap, as you term it, in England.

I am unique.'

The sergeant was still inclined to complain. 'But we was coming along so nice, sir. He's almost stopped going to his office now and have you noticed how his walks take him near the cemetery? He's a guilty man, just as you said.'

'We need facts and we haven't any. He rammed *that* down my throat the other morning. There.' The inspector smoothed his sidewhiskers and buttoned his coat up to the chin. 'How do I look?' Now that the moment had come to leave, his little office looked cosy and the fire bright and inviting. He ran his cuff over the surface of his desk, lovingly.

'Er, there's just one other thing.' He coloured slightly. 'I haven't told my wife.'

'Haven't told your wife you're going to London?' The sergeant was astounded.

'No, bless her, she's made it rather awkward. I just happened to mention I might be going the other day and she went off into floods of tears - wouldn't speak to me for the rest of the day. I don't know what it is with me, Sergeant - I've noticed that other people's wives tend to cool their ardour with the passage of years. Mine has swung the other way. Dashed inconvenient at times - the girls take their cue from mother, if she cries they cry. You've no idea of the wailing that goes on in our house sometimes. I remember when the canary died - I wouldn't live through that again for ten years' salary.' He cheered up. 'So I smuggled my shirts and whatnot out and have written her a letter explaining all. Just drop it in at the door and make a run for it.'

The sergeant groaned.

'Be very grave and business like won't you? No, she'll think somethings happened to me. Say "With Inspector Trumper's compliments and best love" will you?'

'Yes, sir.'

'Be sure to remember "best love".' The inspector's eye was moist. 'For I do love her you know. Ah me.'

EIGHT

With the grey light came the calling of the rooks from the elm trees. In the meadow that ran alongside the quarry path a fox stirred. He sniffed the air and grinned, then trotted off in search of breakfast. Small birds flitted in and out of the hedgerow. Below the ridge the red deer browsed. Somewhere a dog barked.

A boy came limping along the quarry path. A tramping boy, his green jacket torn, his grey breeches gashed to the knee and showing the white of his thigh. Straw, the relics of last night's bed, still clung to his person. His boots, caked with red mud and split, showed too plainly the results of the long miles he had come. A magpie flew across his path.

'Magpie, magpie, flutter and flee . . .' muttered Redemption and looked anxiously for its fellow. Everyone knew it was unlucky to see only one. There it was, a splash of black and white in the meadow, jerking its head back and forth as it walked. He sighed with relief and began to think of food.

Hardship had not dampened Redemption Greenbank's spirit. Rather had it emphasised his natural stubbornness and determination. It was plain to see as he walked, something to do with the purposeful gait, the thrust of his lower lip, his steady gaze. Even so, he cast a glance or two over his shoulder as he went along as if he half expected to see someone. Many days had passed since he last saw Cropper but he had not stopped believing he would meet him soon. The snow was gone, underfoot was thick and miry.

Luckily a period of mild weather had set in; even so, each night was an adventure and his main preoccupation food. He had begged from door to door as he passed and had been, in the main, kindly used. At the big houses the cook or maid had taken pity on him and leant over the half-door watching him eat. They laughed at his accent, called him Irish, asked him if he was a Catholic. In other places they set the dogs on him and called him hard names. He had slept in barns, under bridges, beside ruins, beneath the stars. Cropper's gift of fire had kept his life, his own determination sustained it.

This morning the early sun was touching the dead bracken along the ridge. Redemption left the path and struck upward, he wanted to stand in the sun; the height would enable him to see the lie of the land and plot his day's journey. As he scrambled he could hear a dog barking near at hand, it was difficult to place where it came from but he guessed it was a farm dog somewhere. Near the crest of the ridge was a sort of plateau or shelf and he paused here to catch his breath. He had climbed perhaps eight hundred feet and the land fell away sharply beneath him. Below was the path he had left running along the valley bottom, a river meandered between green water meadows and the other side of the valley, thickly wooded, rose steeply away. Behind this hill, pressing close, were the rounded heights of many more; dark they were with heather or tawny with bracken. This was a land of valleys, of wooded combes, of the red deer.

The barking was louder here but he could see no dog. Puzzled, he looked about, upward and downward, but no animal could he spy. The barking had taken on a new, impassioned note which awakened his interest. Then his eye fell on a bush ten yards away and he realised, with horror, that the notes issued from beneath it. He was a superstitious boy and his first impulse was to turn back down the hill. He was in a strange land; several times at night his slumbers had been broken by mysterious grunts and barkings. There was no way of knowing what this place contained of – fairy, boggle, or elf. But the barking tugged at his heart, it was excited, pleading.

Redemption made his decision, spat to the four points of the compass for luck, and went forward to investigate. He advanced haltingly until he was close enough to see the fissure that opened beneath the bush, no more than two feet across and looking like the lair of some savage goblin. He dropped to his belly and inched forward. A cold damp smell, as of moss and underground water, issued from the mouth of the hole. He called out and the barking redoubled in fury, followed by the sound of scrabbling at the earth, of falling stones, then only a pitiful whimpering. So that was it.

'Poor lost thing,' said Redemption softly to himself, and then, loudly, 'Tis a'reet boy. Poor lad – I'll get ye up.'

He struck one of Cropper's precious matches and peered down. There was nothing but the steep sides of the hole and their wetness. Somewhere water dripped. He could not see the bottom nor the dog who was now whimpering continually.

Redemption made more soothing noises to the animal. 'I'll get ye up!' he promised.

He took off his shirt and jacket; tying one sleeve of the shirt about the bush he knotted the other to his jacket. He now had a rude rope; the hole, he reasoned, could not be too deep as he could hear the dog so closely. Without hesitation he swung himself into it. At once he set off a small avalanche of stones and earth; he braced his back and his knees against the sides of the hole and inched downward like a young chimney sweep. The gloom was profound but as the hole widened he could see the dog's eyes glittering red beneath him.

'There's a good lad,' he said, inwardly hoping that the animal was not so far gone with fear to bite him. 'Soon have you out of this.'

Quite how this was to be done he was not sure, he had hoped that the inspiration of the moment would carry him through. The hole was now so wide that he would have to trust the whole of his weight to his rope. He did so; there was at once the horrid sound of ripping and he landed, quite softly on the floor of the cave.

The dog greeted him with joy, licking his face, pawing at him, moving round and round in the restricted space so swiftly that Redemption began to suspect there might be two of him.

He was winded, but not badly so; above, the little circle of light seemed very far away.

He put on his jacket. There was a sleeve of his shirt attached to it, but the rest of that garment, he reasoned, must be about the bush. If he stood up he could not touch the sides of the hole. It was as if he had been dropped into a bottle; he could see no way of climbing back from where he came.

His heart sank. He remembered how a spider in a bottle ran round and round, frantic for escape. At least the spider had the advantage of being the better climber. The dog, considering itself rescued, pressed against his legs and snuffled. His coat was rough and soft. It was an odd chance that had brought them together. He thought of the dog trapped in this hole in the ground and of himself locked in Slattery's attic. He squatted on his haunches and the animal pushed at him, licking his face all over.

Redemption laughed softly and caressed the curly head.

'Chance,' he said aloud, 'that's all it is.'

Even talking aloud reminded him of Slattery's attic. Chance if he hadn't gone to the cemetery that day. 'And if I hadn't left the path just now, hey?' He patted the dog, 'Why, we might never ha' met, thee and me.'

His being born was just chance. What was it they said when a bitch gave birth to mongrel puppies? Chance-bred. He was chance-bred too; just like this poor trapped cur.

'Most like someone put thee in here, lad,' he said softly, 'I know what it is to be left alone – lost and empty and frightened. But I'll stand thy friend same as Cropper stood by me. We'll get ourselves out of this.'

Somewhere he could hear that most solitary of sounds, water dripping. With remarkable composure he felt in his pockets for a match. He could have cried, or beat the ground, or shouted with all his strength and been hoarse within ten minutes. But Redemption had learned quickly; nothing was so bad, as Cropper might say, without it gets better.

The cave, for such it was, was bigger than had first appeared. He explored its furthest recesses. One wall was of solid rock which looked cold and clammy, black damp and covered in mosses. From here there was a passage leading off; it was shored up with timber, obviously the work of human hands. He remembered the quarry and guessed he must be in its workings somewhere. There was hope yet. The air coming from the passage laid a cold hand on his heart, it smelt dead. As far as he could make out this shaft would lead him downward. He recrossed the floor of the cave, passing the dim pool of light shed by the hole in the roof. On the opposite side he discovered another hole or opening. Perhaps then, the cave was no more than a chamber in a shaft.

And, he thought, if t'other leads down. This must take me up.

Perhaps he imagined it but the air here seemed fresher. He determined to explore further.

If the cave was dark this passage was as black as a wolf's throat. He decided to conserve his matches and make his way by feeling along the walls of the tunnel. He had made some way before he realised that the dog, who previously had twined himself in and out of his legs in a highly dangerous manner, was no longer with him. He sighed and looked back; two red points of light glimmered at him from the safety of the cave. Wearily he went back the way he had come and dragged the dog along with him. The animal was shivering and Redemption's ill-temper melted away.

'It's a'reet lad, I'll get thee out.' He stroked him soothingly and was rewarded with a lick on the hand. The dog's nose was cold and wet; evidently he had had sufficient to drink. Keeping one hand on the scruff of his neck and the other feeling ahead, Redemption stumbled onward. They made a snail's progress. The shaft had been unused a long time, littered with shale and bigger rocks; the wood of the shoring timber felt damp and mossy. The extreme darkness made it difficult to establish what headway they made but his breathing was becoming laboured and sweat trickled into the small of his back. He was sure they were climbing upward but look back or forward he could see nothing but the palpable blackness that pressed against his eyes.

'Can't be much further,' he said aloud, with more hope than conviction, and listening to the echoing of his voice. 'Eh, lad? Chance – that's what I'll call thee – Chance is a good name.' He felt the dog's contours. 'Chance is a good name for a long dog.' He didn't add, with instinctive delicacy, that it may have been an ill chance that brought them together. 'We'll soon be out, Chance.'

For a time this happy outcome hung in the balance. Their way was barred by a heavy fall of earth and stone. Through the small gap that was left he could see daylight and the entrance to the shaft but try as he may he could make little impression on the blockage before him. His nails broke and his fingers bled as he attempted to dislodge the heavy stones which were cemented together by damp and impacted earth. Despair had begun to creep into his heart when the light was blocked by a figure at the mouth of the tunnel who called out to him. In moments the expert use of two or three spades had forced a hole big enough for him to crawl through. He was led blinking into the light.

He found himself the centre of attention in a group of labourers. They stood or sprawled about him on the hillside, their picks by them, smoking or eating. Fortunately for Redemption, the quarrymen had chosen this spot by his tunnel to eat their bait. The foreman, a man with huge whiskers and a cider-drinker's complexion, did most of the talking.

'That's Jem Maddocks' dog,' he observed.

'Daft as a squirrel,' someone enjoined mildly. A snicker of laughter ran through the group. They were big, gentle men; most of them wore corduroy trousers tied at the knee with string and heavy hobnailed boots. They smoked their pipes and looked down at the pair before them with interest but no alarm.

'Must've bin down Black Hole on the ridge there. Chasing rabbits was 'ee?'

Before Redemption could answer he was interrupted.

'Jem swore blind 'ee done away with that dog this Friday gone.'

'Where's Jem to?'

'Hard labour. He was caught red-handed in Cutcombe with two brace of pheasants.'

There was another snicker of laughter; no one seemed particularly sorry for Jem. They eyed Redemption with amusement and asked him if he was 'one of Jem's'. He explained what had happened and they whistled and shook their heads, saying it was a bad thing to throw a dog down a hole – Jem weren't no good, never was since a boy. The area, they explained, was littered with old workings, man traps – he was lucky.

The foreman tossed the dog a crust and watched him bolt it.

'Here my lad,' he said kindly, and gave the rest of his scraps to him. 'If you've been down Black Hole since Friday you must be near starved.'

Perhaps Redemption's face showed more than it ought for a swarthy little labourer with a jerky head thrust a piece of fat bacon in his hand and intimated that he too should eat.

'Thank you, mister,' Redemption bit the meat clean in two with his sharp teeth, giving half to the dog who swallowed it whole and licked his hand. It seemed to delight the quarrymen more than anything else he could have done; they plied them both with more bread and cheese.

'This Jem, he won't come looking for his dog will he?'

'They give him three munce,' replied the swarthy labourer. 'Don't you worry yourself. He's locked up, me dear – you take the dog on. He's took a fancy to you and no wonder.'

'He were a poaching sort of man?' asked Redemption thoughtfully.

'He were,' replied another, puffing at his pipe. 'A terrible cruel one too. Never saw him use a muzzle on his ferrets, not Jem. Used to sew their lips together.'

Redemption knelt on the heather and scratched behind the dog's ear. 'Thou reckons I might keep him then?' he asked shyly.

It was the common view of the group that if he did not the animal would starve.

'What would you call him?' The foreman asked, 'Jem

weren't one for pet names. Barring a cuss or two I don't expect this animal ever had a name.'

Redemption kept his eyes on the dog. 'I thought Chance.'

Considering the way he'd come by him Chance would do well enough, they said. They showed him the way out of the quarry and he left them with a feeling of real regret. They were kindly men and completely without curiosity.

Chance led the way in transports of joy, dashing through the ruined bracken on the hillside, snapping at his tail, rejoining the path and waiting for Redemption to catch up, capering, glad to be alive. He was a lurcher, a rough-coated long dog bred for poaching, for driving hares and rabbits into the long net on moonless nights, for taking a plump pheasant or partridge or any other game, so long as it wasn't legal. He could, Redemption saw, be a dangerous companion, but, used wisely, an invaluable one.

He soon proved this. Redemption was cold without his shirt and decided to retrieve it when he found himself upon the road he had taken earlier in the morning. Back up the ridge they climbed, Chance in the lead, on the alert, ears pricked. Before they attained the plateau the dog was worming forward on his belly. Perhaps hunger sharpened his reactions and his instincts, for when Redemption reached the same spot he was in time to see his dog trotting back, the limp body of a rabbit between his jaws.

'Thou art a jewel!' breathed Redemption. It wasn't a fat rabbit but it was meat. Expertly he paunched it, tossing the belly and guts onto the grass for the dog to eat at once. He would roast it over an open fire he decided.

It was a long time cooking and when it did come it was burnt on the outside and raw in the middle. A pinch of salt wouldn't have hurt it either but it was worth waiting for for all that. Chance had the head and forelegs, the boy the back and back legs.

Meat put new heart and life in the pair of them. It wasn't begged meat, other men's scraps and leavings, but meat they had won for themselves. They worried each scrap, stripping every particle of meat and tendon from each bone and then exploring it for more. If the eating was over too soon, boy and dog were satisfied, with food and with each other. Chance lolled on his back and allowed his belly to be scratched, hind leg twitching. He watched Redemption through half-closed lids. From that moment his life belonged to the boy.

Freedom was now a prize worth having. Their supply of food was more regular even if they didn't catch meat every day. More important, there was companionship and high spirits. Chance was the eternal optimist ready to chase anything that moved. He put up deer, pulled down a hare and missed many more, came into disagreement with a badger one night and got off very lightly with a bitten nose. He quartered every field they crossed, nose to the ground, hope of success burning in his breast. Cats were at dreadful risk, he squabbled with them all and this tendency often did harm to their chances for begged food.

One day his love of mischief landed them in more serious trouble. They came by a farm, a neat and prosperous assembly of buildings with a collection of yard dogs who lay about the gateways watching them pass. Farms were good places to beg so Redemption paused. At once there came a low growl from three or four throats. Chance cringed against Redemption, tail tucked between his legs.

'There's nought for 'ee here – take thy road or I'll have the dogs on 'ee.'

They were being watched by a gross, red-faced countryman who leant over the wall. He waved an ungainly arm in the direction he thought the boy should take and added a few unflattering words about tramping folk and the nuisances they caused.

Redemption wasted no words but continued his way, whistling to show his unconcern. He had gone some way before he realised Chance was not with him. He called once or twice with no result. Then he saw him emerge through the hedge about a hundred yards away and stand waiting. He was wagging his tail and grinning. As the boy approached he turned back into the hedge and commenced dragging and pulling at something. It was a dead hen.

The boy hesitated. Caution and hunger fought it out for a moment and caution lost. He thrust the bird into his jacket and set off at a run. He had got a bare ten yards when a muscular young farm-hand, vaulting the field gate, barred his way. He had seen the whole transaction.

'Neat as ninepence,' he told the farmer, 'whilst you was hollering at the young 'un the dog slipped away and lifted the fowl. More like a fox than a natural dog. I don't reckon the other birds stopped pecking or looked up to see him.' He was lost in admiration. 'That's a dog, that is.'

The farmer was wheezy and red-faced. He cursed profoundly.

'That's a locking-up offence. I've lost too much to you tramping folk. What with you and the foxes I can't keep a fowl on the place. Why when I think 'o it . . .' His rage turned into an uncontrollable fit of coughing that turned his face black. He was obliged to call for a chair. Seated he resembled nothing so much as one of his own porkers with his tiny eyes and enormous belly. When he had got his breath he burst out passionately.

'And now where's that dang dog to?'

It was true. During the commotion Chance had slipped away again unobserved by everyone. His whereabouts were announced almost at once as a fearful barking and yelping broke out in the barn. By the time they reached the door Chance was on his way out dragging an enormous rat. Meekly he laid it at the farmer's feet.

The farmer turned it over with his toe. Nose to tip it must have measured eighteen inches; its lips were drawn back over its teeth and dark blood trickled from its mouth.

'That's a rat,' the farmer allowed. His anger took another direction as he shook his fist at his own dogs. 'See that! Not one of you could catch me such a rat!'

He resumed his chair. 'Plaguey rats.' He looked down at Chance who cringed and grinned at once.

'Tell 'ee what I'll do. I'll take the dog there and we'll say naught else about the lock-up. What do you say to that? If the magistrate has 'ee they'll take the dog anyhow. Drown it I shouldn't wonder.'

He said this last with a snigger.

Redemption swallowed hard.

'Good hens cost money and you've no means to pay.'

'Tell 'ee what I'll do for 'ee – come back this way in a week. If he's cleared the rats you may have him back.'

He said this with real magnanimity for he believed he was being generous. 'That's what I'll do.'

So Redemption was left alone without his dog and with an empty heart. He slunk off but he didn't go far. From the wooded hillside he could look down on the farm until it grew too dark. He sat with his knees drawn-up listening to the sighing of the wind in the larches. The sound matched his mood. The plantation was dark and noiseless, underfoot dead apart from the odd struggling bramble. The poles of the trees were like the masts of the *Lord Henry*. He could be at sea now with the sound of the wind and the creaking of the timber. Did Chance miss him? They had not known each other so very long. He looked a piteous sight as he was led away, tail tucked between his legs, a cringing expression on his face. He certainly wasn't a brave dog but Redemption had grown attached to him and was determined to win him back. He had no plan; his only notion was to sneak down into the farmyard under cover of night and release his dog from the barn. If Cropper was here daresay he might think of a better plan but he wasn't. What would happen if the other dogs raised the alarm and he was caught, he didn't bother to consider. His was a mind that waited for the inspiration of the moment.

The cold empty hours passed by somehow. Afternoon turned into evening, buckets clanked below him in the farmyard, the grunting and squealing of the hogs died away at last. Silence filled the valley.

He got up stiffly. By daylight he had marked his path and he left the wood without hindrance although not without his heart beating a little faster at the prospect before him. He aimed to cross the field behind the barn in the most direct manner and there enter the farmyard. Country people were abed early this time of year, the farmhouse was no more than a dark massy shape from which no light burned. But there was another light, a single unblinking eye set down in the middle of the field he wished to cross. He spat and muttered a charm before keeping to the hedgerow and giving the mysterious light a wide berth. He had no wish to involve himself with goblins and fairies. But it increased his nervousness and it was with terror he heard a low growl at his feet and saw a figure loom at him from the night. A hand was clapped over his mouth and he was pulled to the ground. He lay there without a struggle expecting his throat to be cut but all he heard was a dry chuckle.

''Tis the boy, I've catched him once already today.'

The speaker was the young farm-hand who had apprehended them both earlier in the day. 'Leave, Tig.' This to a wall-eyed farm dog who had Redemption by the breeches.

'I can guess what you're after,' went on the farm-hand softly. 'That sneaking long dog of yourn?'

Redemption swallowed his fear.

'I've got to have him back, mister. I've got to. He's my dog – I can't leave him here. I won't leave till he comes wi' me.'

Something about the young man's silence encouraged him further.

'I was coming to take him now,' he said boldly.

'He showed Tig up today when he took that rat. There's not a smarter dog on this farm than my Tig.'

The young man allowed him to sit up and, being well disposed to Redemption, explained what he was doing. To make amends for Tig's fall from grace he had determined to catch the fox who had been plaguing their chickens lately. It was his own patent theory which, he claimed, worked every time. Foxes, being innately curious creatures, could not resist investigating the source of light.

'Then I shoots 'em,' said the young man modestly. 'Tig pulls 'em down if I don't make a clean hit. All you need is a strong lantern set in the middle of the field. He's a grand dog is Tig. I shouldn't know what I'd do without him.'

This last remark struck him silent for a moment. Jealousy of Chance and feeling for the boy combined to suggest a course of action which would suit them both.

'Master was a mite hard,' he remarked thoughtfully. 'Too hard I'd say. Should us go and see how your dog is getting along?'

There was no alarm as they approached the barn. A dog or two stirred but fell silent as they recognised Tig and the farm-hand. He bade Redemption wait while he eased open the great door. Moments later a grey shadow crossed the yard as stealthily as a fox. Chance licked his hand but contained his excitement with an instinctive sense of the situation.

'Not one rat!' The farm-hand was overjoyed. 'He was laying by the door waiting to be let out. Tig would do better any day. Get off out of it the pair of ye.'

There was not light enough to see the wink that accompanied this.

Three miles further along the road they found a wall that broke the wind. Considering that Chance would not be missed for a while Redemption rested. Even in the dark he could make out the outline of the hills; the trees tossed their heads in an uncanny, ghostly way. He felt very small and alone. Chance was huddled so close to him he could feel the dog's heart beating through his ribs. Redemption combed his fingers through the warm curls, teasing out the burrs and fragments of twig tangled there. 'Thou art my darling,' he whispered. In all his short life he had never used such words; they were awkward in his mouth like stones but immeasurably comforting.

'Thou art my treasure,' he said, over and over again.

NINE

Two days later their wandering life took its final turn. They were sitting at the roadside munching begged bread, idly watching the rooks in the fields, when a carter pulled up and enquired if they wanted a ride. It was a painted waggon and the harness bells jingled as the horse cropped the verge. Redemption never learned the name of the carter, a big man in a smock who smelled like a bag of oats, but the horse's name was Handsome. Handsome allowed himself to be patted but showed a strong inclination to kick Chance. From the safety of the cart Chance taunted Handsome with a bark or two but in the days to come took care never to get too near his hooves.

It was splendid pulling through the lanes that morning, riding where they should have walked, looking out over the wide misty fields. As they grew talking, it turned out that the carter was bound for Watford and his road would take him through London. He offered to carry the pair of them for free, he was a man who liked someone to talk to. He had a brother on a farm in Watford and he was to transact some business there. He had a sister in Canada on a farm, another brother in Australia on a farm, another brother – the black sheep – somewhere off Cape Horn before the mast. In the two days it took them to travel to London Redemption learned all about his children, Rose and Oliver, his terrier Grip, his pet bullfinch Chip. He was a man who never tired of talking about himself or those dear to him and evinced no curiosity about anything else. Listening to him was a small price to pay for watching the long miles slip by and resting weary limbs.

Soon enough the milestones told the distance to London in

single numbers. It seemed to turn dark as they rode into the great city by the West Road, now one among many where before they had been solitary travellers. The waggon had been their home for long enough for both of them to feel a qualm at leaving it. They were engulfed in a rattling throng that pushed onward in a bad-tempered way, continually getting jammed and snarled. It was dog eat dog, observed the carter, ignoring the raised fist of a cabbie whose side he had just shaved. Handsome didn't like it, he tossed his head but the jingle of all his bells was lost in the tumult. Up front a cart had gone over, spilling its load – 'What price cabbage,' said the carter, watching a good part of the produce getting trampled underfoot, 'How do you like London?'

'It's big,' the boy said, wondering.

The carter laughed. 'Big. I'll give you that. What else?'

'Dirty and there's a sight too many folk. How do they all live?'

'Anyhow,' responded the carter, nonchalantly taking his waggon through a gap where no waggon should go, 'Topsy-turvy. Taddywhack and tandem as my wife's old mother would say. Are you still sure you want me to set you down?'

'I must meet my friend,' Redemption said, taking a tighter hold of Chance.

'We have been easy together,' remarked the carter, 'what say you come on to Watford with me?'

'Thankee, mister. I must meet him where he said.'

'A good friend?'

'The best I could ever have.'

The carter did not laugh this time. 'Let us find somewhere to put you down then.'

A big dirty place, buildings as tall as cliffs and a sea of pale thronging faces beneath them. It was a tide that muttered restlessly, swirling every way at once – off the pavements, down turnings, through archways, out of shops, into hotels and out again. Redemption swallowed hard and watched it all. He had never seen so many tall black hats at once, bobbing about like gulls on the water. The street-sellers in all their variety took the eye, if only because the cart narrowly avoided crushing so many of them. They paraded their wares in the roadway, shouting and calling above the din all manner of curious things; cures for shingles and heartburn, pies, buttons, hot potatoes, confessions of murderers before they were hanged, fruit, flowers, chickweed for canaries, tracts. Their breath smoking in the raw air.

He was set down somewhere, Chance plunging at every passerby in the expectation of being greeted as a long lost friend. He was tied with string but it had little effect on his sociable impulses. They made their staggering way somehow, feeling that they had been set adrift, that everyone had a fixed destination except for themselves, everyone a fixed purpose, everyone a fixed expression of going somewhere in a hurry. They were buffeted this way and that, turning with the tide, being carried along and swept who knows where until Redemption, after several fruitless attempts, caught a tall black hat's attention and enquired the way to Covent Garden.

It was 'That way,' the man flung a hasty arm, 'not very far.'

Big shops with enough plate glass to build several fairy-tale palaces, the shoppers very regal. He watched a lady being handed up into her conveyance while another attendant struggled behind with a huge pot plant which waved over her head fanning her.

'Out of the way! Look sharp!' Two more men in green baize aprons staggered to a furniture van which they were loading with chairs and tables.

So this was London. He had heard of it as the place where the queen lived much as he had heard of heaven as the place God lived. A sooty city, a place that made you cough and gave you a headache. All the buildings in black, frowning down, very conscious of their superiority as if to say 'you are very small and we are so very big'. Everyone milling about, shouting and calling, clattering, whistling, every one of them knowing where they were and where they were going.

He found Covent Garden as the lamps were being lit. A place with arches, crowded with barrows, baskets and stalls.

The first thing he noticed, apart from the overwhelming smell of cabbage, was that the people here were more on his level; he felt more comfortable among the noisy costers, the ragged children picking over the rubbish and lurking in the shadows, the old women collecting stray fragments of greens. He picked up a rotten apple from the gutter and ate it. Chance worried a cabbage stump and the men pushing barrows told him, jovially, to 'mind his eye', as if he had the right to be there. He liked the costers. By the flaring lamps they looked a bold bunch; they set their caps at a rakish angle, didn't bother with coats but wore waistcoats with brass buttons and flaunting neckerchiefs. They were cheerfully loud, calling and laughing, swearing at their donkeys as they pushed and pulled impossible loads, everything done with a swagger and with good humour.

A fair amount of this good humour could be set down to the number of public houses in the vicinity. As evening progressed their doors swung open with increasing frequency, the smell of tobacco smoke and spirits did battle with the cabbage. The Black Cat was crammed to the door by the time he found it, the market people passing drink to one another over their heads. He tied Chance to a lamppost and ventured in. It was warm work getting to the bar but he was small and could go where a grown man couldn't. They were busy and it was a job to get their attention, a balding man, who wore a fancy waistcoat and two young women, who continually pushed back stray hair from their flushed faces as they served the beer. It was one of them who noticed his steady young gaze after he had been waiting some ten minutes and bent down to him.

Cropper? The name went from mouth to mouth and there was a general shaking of heads. He owed someone two pun' fifteen, Cropper was a shocker, but as to his whereabouts they were blowed if they knew. Try 'Far Mulvanny' someone said. Yes, that was it 'Far Mulvanny' good idea. The conversation turned to someone else.

Outside rain fell slowly through the gaslight like snow. Chance was wet, shook himself furiously, jumped up with his tail wagging ready to be off. But where to? He cast a doubtful eye at the shadowy arches hearing the chattering voices of the street urchins. Should he throw in his lot with them? Survival did not worry him, but should he wait for Cropper here or go and look for him? He didn't know where this Far Mulvanny was and London was a big place.

'Are you the fellow asking for Cropper?'

He looked up. The speaker was a youngish man who wore no hat and was dressed in an odd, long black garment which reached to his toes. He wore spectacles and carried a black book with ribbons in it close to his chest.

'I'm Father Mulvanny. I couldn't get to ye in there – you see I was engaged in earnest conversation, earnest ...' He broke off, eyes twinkling behind the glasses, chuckling foolishly. 'Ah, but it's thirsty work working in the old market all day.' He chuckled again as if he was repressing laughter. Father Mulvanny nodded at him, oblivious of the rain which dripped from his hair on to his spectacles, 'Thirsty work,' he repeated.

' 'Ere guv'nor, give us a treat.' Two urchins had approached and watched from a distance.

Father Mulvanny searched his pockets. 'Do you know boys, I haven't a brass farthing, not a penny.'

'Drunk it all 'ave you?' they asked, not without sympathy.

'I drink only water, crystal water, the purest drink of all, as the song has it,' replied Father Mulvanny and burst into foolish laughter.

'Dun't you wear funny clothes?'

'I do, I do indeed,' Father Mulvanny laughed again as if this was choice wit. 'I'm a man of God you see –'

'God A'mighty,' said one.

'God save the Queen,' said the other.

'That's who I mean,' agreed the priest. 'And what do ye know of God?'

''E made the world,' said one promptly.

''Oo done the houses?' asked his friend.

'Ah, I expect the working people did that – the building,' replied Father Mulvanny.

'Then there's Jesus,' went on the knowledgeable one. 'He's

Our Saviour – he said if anyone was to go and 'it you you wasn't to slosh 'im back.'

'Blimey! I should like to see anyone try, that's all!' exclaimed his friend indignantly.

'You're terrible fellows, are ye not? Whoever had the saving of you would have his work cut out.' The priest laughed, the picture of delight, with the rain falling harder on his bare head and the drops glinting on his glasses. The two urchins crept nearer to the circle of light. 'But where do you learn about Jesus?'

'Down at the 'all. They give you a cup of tea and tells you about Our Saviour.'

'He'd be glad you had the cup of tea,' observed the priest approvingly.

'What's his lay?' demanded the talkative one, at a tangent, pointing to Redemption. 'Never seen 'im afore. 'Im and 'is dog.'

Father Mulvanny brought his attention back to Redemption.

'That's a very thin dog. Very thin indeed and all this rain does nothing for his looks – come on out of the wet a moment. Now then you two terrible men, what are your names?'

Billy and, it sounded like, Stovvy.

'Well Billy and er, Stovvy. Next time you see me I'll give ye a penny. Go on now and find somewhere out of the rain I want to have a private talk with this young man here. Mind ye be kind to one another!' He watched them glide away into the shadows and shook his head. There was no clue to his thoughts in the sudden determined thrust of his jaw.

'Cropper was one of my flock.' Noticing Redemption's blank expression he added, 'I'm a Catholic priest, Cropper was one of my parishioners. There are a lot of Irish hereabouts and some English Catholics too – like Cropper. I always liked Cropper even though he was out of one scrape and into another before you could turn round. I had high hopes for him – I heard he was courting a Catholic girl in Liverpool.'

'He's run away.' Redemption filled in the details for the priest whose face lengthened during the telling.

'He's not been to London for a twelvemonth – and you've nowhere to go. Sure, all this is as strange to you as it once was to me fresh from Ballyduff. Ye've a country boy's complexion – did ye not see how pale those two were under all that grime? It isn't air we breathe here but sulphur – sure we'd be better off on the slopes of a volcano, we would indeed –' He paused as a man loomed by and stopped.

'I'm off home this minute, father. Are ye content? I said it was just the couple.'

Father Mulvanny's face brightened again as he took the man by the sleeve. Redemption did not have to be very quick to guess that this was something to do with the earnest conversation mentioned earlier. 'Oh good man, Michael. I promised the wife you'd be home early tonight. Good night now, mind how ye go – avoid the snares and temptations of Owd Nick along the way.'

The man guffawed and gave them good night. Father Mulvanny looked up at the sky. 'The rain is easing a little, I think.'

Redemption couldn't see that it was.

'What's your name? Redemption? Lord have mercy it's an old Puritan you are. Don't you think Dick would have been easier to live with? Mind you my own name is a precious mouthful, Aloysius – what do ye think of that? I always wanted to be called Kevin when I was a lad.' Father Mulvanny studied the pavement benevolently as they walked along. 'Ye've an interesting face, Redemption. A man's face is an open book if ye've an eye to see what's written there. Now, I'd say you were a stoic – not that ye'd understand me – but it's no bad thing to be. It's a good face ye have, Redemption. We'll have a fine old natter when we get home.'

Father Mulvanny lived by the river and looked out of the window at the spars and rigging of ocean-going vessels. He said the air was almost as fresh as Ballyduff's. It needed to be if only to counteract the fetid stench of the warrens and alleys in which he spent his days. He led the boy through the gutters splashing them both liberally as he rattled along, waving to people he knew, ignoring the odd ribald remark. He was the happiest man Redemption had ever met.

'Now there, ye can smell the river bringing up great gobfulls of fresh air from the sea.' He banged his chest appreciatively. "'Tis like living at the seaside – though not so dull.'

A curious seaside. The river moved oilily beneath the shadows of great warehouses, barely stirring the rows of barges, making the lights wink. Perhaps Redemption had not got used to it yet but the smell was none of the sweetest.

Father Mulvanny's house was in a side street next door to a chandler's and presided over by Mrs O'Hare.

'Jesus, Mary and Joseph,' said that lady. 'What have ye dragged home this time?'

She led them through to where the fire burned, she had been dozing there herself not a moment before and a stimulating smell of spirits still pervaded the air.

'Another mouth for dinner I suppose – two mouths, get down ye daft whelp. Come and have a warm by the fire.' She motioned, not unkindly, for Redemption to come forward into the fire glare.

Father Mulvanny sat in a creaking armchair and took off his boots. 'Is Jimmy home?' he asked.

In reply there was a rumble of wheels from another room at which Chance took fright and barked. A legless man, who looked almost like half a man, pushed himself forward on a crude wooden trolley.

'Very good, father, nearly made thirty shillings.'

'If ye'd told me five pounds I wouldn't have been surprised.' Father Mulvanny gazed at a hole in his socks and wriggled his toes in the heat. 'Now Redemption – Jimmy, this is a friend of Cropper's – give me your opinion of this wooden soldier.' He took one down from the mantleshelf.

'Let him keep it,' said Jimmy.

'Ah, Jim, it's more ruthless you should be. Our great capitalists didn't found their fortunes by giving away their stock in trade.'

'Ruthless yourself,' muttered Mrs O'Hare as she moved about the room preparing the table, 'Giving away our good dinner to Protestants.'

'Now, Redemption, did ye ever see the like of it? The Duke of Wellington - old Boney himself - never commanded a more handsome rifleman than that one. Correct in every detail - Jimmy should know. It's works of art they are, to my mind, works of art.'

After dinner, at Mrs O'Hare's instigation, Redemption was bathed before the fire. While she brought up jug after jug of steaming water, Father Mulvanny sat and read from his black book with the ribbons in it. Even after the boy was dry, the reading continued. He yawned in an old broken-backed chair by the fire, Chance curled at his feet, relishing the warmth and shelter of the priest's room. Neither Mrs O'Hare nor Father Mulvanny were too particular in respect of dust but it was comfortable enough. Apart from a crucifix over the fireplace there was no obvious object of piety there.

'Now,' said the priest, closing his book at last, 'that's done. The question now is what's to be done for you? eh? As far as I can make out you and Cropper jumped ship and ran away - is that it? Running away seems to be in Cropper's line these days and we must have sharp words together when we meet. Until that day you may stay here - Jimmy is leaving us shortly so we have the room - owd Mrs O'Hare is a splendid creature at heart and she'll give ye a shakedown. If Cropper doesn't show up - if he's kept on running - no, I can see by your face you don't believe that. I can see that I've been making you sit with me when ye should be sleeping - it's thoughtless I am - it's bed for now.'

Two or three days passed with Father Mulvanny. The priest's parish seemed to be in the streets he spent such long hours tramping. Once he was rested, Redemption found it irksome to stay with Mrs O'Hare and asked one morning to accompany the priest. The suggestion was received with relief on the part of the lady, who found the boy a constraint on her naps by the fire, and with pleasure by Father Mulvanny. He had grown to like Redemption more with each day; he saw with admiration that he laboured under a great secret but kept it staunchly, unflinchingly. He forebore to press him on it; all the boy's faith was pinned on Cropper, who must have done something remarkable to deserve it.

'This is a great city, indeed it is,' he observed as they walked by the shopmen sweeping the pavements, taking down the shutters, trimming the lamps. Already the life of the street was in full bustle, hallowed by a pale morning sun that would wane before noon. 'I'm sure God must look down and see it as one great anthill, each of us crawling on top of the other, each of us set on our own little purpose, a heaving, teeming mass.' He waved an airy hand, 'Ants, that's all we are. Very little. And we are bound in our little way to Feeney's the letter writer for they told me after Mass that he was bad. Do you mind if I sing?'

He sang most of *Barbara Allen* as they walked along. Redemption had nothing to do but listen, Father Mulvanny's voice was inclined to crack here and there but when he was asked what he thought he replied, 'Very good.'

'Yes,' agreed the priest complacently, 'I think I manage it expressively, I think I do. When I was a lad I sang at all the weddings near Ballyduff and I have an enormous repertoire, I do indeed, though no one but Mrs O'Hare gets to hear it these days.

'Not today thank you,' to a blind man who proferred a tray of matches. 'Nor tomorrow if I can help it, ye skulking old villain, ye precious old rip,' he added in an undertone.

Father Mulvanny laughed at Redemption's startled expression.

'I'm short of Christian charity in that direction,' he said, 'that's Blind John Shaw the Scotsman and he's a pair of eyes better than my own. Pah! He's got a mate who poses as a one-legged man – he keeps his good leg strapped up and uses crutches to get about. It makes my blood boil, sure it does, when there's a man like Jimmy, who lost both legs to a cannon-ball, and who will beg for nothing. Nothing. Those wooden soldiers he carves are not objects for charity, he could make a living selling those if his pins were as nimble as your own.'

He explained how Jimmy came to be at his house, how he had been brought there more dead than alive from starvation, how he had recovered and struck out a living for himself. Father Mulvanny didn't mention that the wooden soldier project was his own idea nor that he paid for Jimmy's tools.

'There's terrible tragedy in these streets. Tragedy that daily rubs shoulders with villainy – can ye wonder how good men go to the bad? That man there now – don't stare – the one selling postcards in the street. That man used to be a clergyman and he lost his living through no fault of his own, no fault at all. He speaks Latin better than I do, look at him selling postcards – ach, and then I think of Blind John Shaw and his ilk. But come, we're nearly at Feeney's and I meant to buy you a currant bun – here's a pastrycook's.'

They left the main thoroughfare and were in an untidy area littered with rubbish and hung with washing. They were at the back of an eating-house and the steamy smell of boiled greens mingled with the clatter of pans and the sound of sizzling fat as the day's dinners got under way.

Feeney had a room above this establishment which was reached by climbing an outside staircase. Even by the dingy light that strained through the dirty windows, it was plain Feeney was in a bad way. Redemption waited outside with his currant bun and Chance.

'Well, Feeney, how is it?'

Bad.

Father Mulvanny sat on the bed and took Feeney's wasted, yellowing hand in his. 'Have ye a doctor?'

The doctor was coming but he needed a priest worse than a doctor – it was the letters . . .

'Ach, Feeney people never believed in them. Any money you had from them was charity,' Father Mulvanny took his rumpled purple stole from his pocket.

'The lies!' muttered Feeney.

'No one believed in them at all. It was bad in ye but you had no benefit from them at all. Still . . .' Father Mulvanny kissed the stole and put it about his neck with a sigh.

When he came out it was with a serious countenance, 'The man hasn't long.' He observed, looking down into the area, 'This is a miserable beginning for ye, Redemption. I had hoped for a better start to the day. I shall have to bring him the Sacrament. Ach, poor devil, he's a long way from Sligo and no one will know of his passing. He said he thought he could hear the beat of the ocean on Cummeen Strand, poor soul . . .' Father Mulvanny drifted off into thought. 'I must go back to the chapel for the Sacrament,' he said after an interval. 'When I return I must speak to no one as I carry it – as a mark of reverence, you understand – I will be quicker if I go alone. Can ye wait here until I return?'

It was agreed. Father Mulvanny counselled him against talking to strangers and against wandering too far. He promised he would not be above an hour.

He had been left in a neighbourhood of pawnbrokers and old clothes shops. The fact that Feeney lay dying meant little to him; he finished his bun, tossing a scrap to the dog, and thought about his life. It didn't amount to much, not too many people would care if he died either. Cropper would be sorry, Slattery would be glad. He shivered as he thought of himself alone in the attic room with Slattery. Mad Slattery who said he meant you no harm while looking at you with eyes which plainly showed that life and death were alike to him. Mad Slattery whose giant shadow danced on the wall in the candle-light and dwarfed his life even now.

'We may not meet again . . .' that's what he had said.

If they did meet again after what he had told Cropper, if ever he was in Slattery's power again after running away . . . He put his hand on Chance burying his fingers in the warm fur, Chance turned his head to look him full in the eye. unblinking.

'That's a fine dog.' He didn't much like the look of the man who stopped to speak but he agreed with pride.

'I bet he could catch a rabbit, that one.'

'Aye.'

'Let's have a look at his teeth,' abruptly the man leant forward and in a markedly brutal way gripped Chance's mouth with one hand while turning back his lip with the other. 'A fine set of gnashers,' he said, after a detailed inspection. 'He could rip and gouge if you give him the chance, yah – get away.'

He shoved Chance away and stood up. He was dressed as a working man but there was something out of the ordinary in the brutal cast of his features. His lank yellow hair framed a face that looked as though it had been carved out of something hard.

'What's 'is name?' He mis-heard it. 'Chas, Chas, come here.'

Chance did, fawning and sniffing, excitedly. The man let him lick his hands all over, eyeing him all the time. Redemption, suddenly afraid, called him back but Chance ignored him, wagging his tail at his new friend.

'He likes me. Yes, I'm all right you can trust me.' He allowed the dog to sniff his body before pushing his face away in the same brutal manner. 'He don't want to know you now, do he?' He ran his hand over the arch of Chance's back, noting the thick hard muscle on the thighs.

'Go away, boy.' But he didn't mean it, there was something cruel and exulting about his tone.

Chance wouldn't leave him alone. Redemption had left off his lead and there was no way to get him back. The man laughed at his efforts.

'He wants to come along of me. Come on, Chas.' He walked away a few paces, Chance following as if he was bewitched, tail wagging slavishly.

The man halted. 'Tell you what,' he said, taking something from his pocket, 'why don't you give 'im to me?'

Redemption was stunned. 'No,' he managed.

'That's too bad,' said the man, with a laugh. 'That's too bad 'cause I'm having him just the same.' He slipped a leash over Chance's head. 'C'mon, Chas, you come wiv me. As for you, my boy –'

SPONGE & S

Redemption received a sudden stinging blow to the head.
'You'll feel the weight of my hand worse if you kick up. You run along home.' He thrust his hard face at Redemption and bent a terrible glance on him. 'I'm a bad man when I'm roused.'

With one more callous laugh he made away.

Numbed, Redemption watched them go.

'Stop!'

No one paid any attention. 'That's my dog!' Tears started in his eyes, why would no one help? 'He's mine!'

If he didn't do something Chance would be gone for ever. He began to run, following blindly down a twisting, crowded alley until panting he came up with the dog-stealer.

'Thief! Dirty thief!' The man swung round but Redemption was ready for him. He ducked under the blow and grabbed at his waist with both arms. The man let out an oath as he found himself hampered by the dog who set off barking and tugging at his leash, the enchantment over. The dog thief staggered back pushing the boy away with his free hand. Chance commenced darting and snapping at his ankles, for an instant Redemption found a substantial portion of the man's wrist between his teeth and bit hard. The leash tangled about their legs until they stumbled and staggered over into a kicking and writhing heap in the gutter.

The man was first to his feet, his face black with rage. He kicked Chance so hard the dog was lifted bodily off the ground for the space of two yards. Chance, yelping grievously, retired limping, taking no further part in the affray. The man turned to Redemption.

There is no knowing what violence might have ensued for just at that moment an officer of the law, attracted by the cries, ran out of a pawnbroker's shop.

TEN

The main hall of the police station was more like the concourse of a railway station than anything else. Everyone seemed to be booking in, or waiting for someone to arrive, or studying the printed notices, or trying to snatch some sleep on a bench. A more careful study revealed that many were the worse for drink, inclined to be abusive, or stolidly sullen. All regarded the uniformed staff with ill-concealed resentment even while protesting their innocence or honesty in ardent tones. Down the passage, out of sight, there was a clanging of doors and a voice announced that he was going to keep banging his head until someone did something. After this a jovial voice would be heard advising him, from time to time, to 'keep banging'.

A gentleman, obviously lost, who had been studying the printed lists of missing persons and the other notices of wanted persons, and the lists of missing jewellery and rewards, turned around and looked for someone to do something. But the uniformed staff just smiled a smile which said, 'Bless you sir, we ain't wet behind the ears. We know what's what. Next please.'

Next was Redemption and the hard-faced dog thief. A policeman, breathing hard with the beginnings of a black eye, attended by several young men in the second-hand clothes trade who had assisted in the arrest and had come along for some more fun, made up the rest of the party. Chance had crawled under a nearby bench.

Case was this. Man and boy in fierce argument over ownership of dog, said dog – where was dog? – (Chance dragged forward) said dog, according to witnesses, evinced partiality to both, answered to the name of Chas or Chance. Man particularly violent, give me this shiner – policeman touched his eye, tried not to notice the slow grin of the officer at the desk – would like to charge him with something, resisting arrest, striking an officer of the law, anything would do.

A torrent of protest from Redemption and the hard-faced man. The policeman on the desk lay down his pen with a sigh and commanded them to speak one at a time beginning with the boy.

Redemption spoke, hotly and at some length.

The policeman sighed again.

'So young 'un' this is your dog. This individual whose face is against 'im for starters – come along and took your dog?'

'And brayed me!' said Redemption indignantly, eyeing the dog thief.

'You mean 'e 'it you? Bright red mark on your 'ead is where 'e 'it you?'

'What about this here, then?' burst out the dog thief passionately, thrusting his dirty wrist beneath the policeman's nose, 'What is that if it is not blood – my blood? What are those marks if they are not teeth-marks – his teeth?' He appealed to the rest of the room as one free-born Englishman to another, 'He got that bang on his head trying to bite me. I was defending myself! There is no one in this room who would allow himself to be *bit*!'

'Very good, thank you very much,' broke in the policeman drily. 'We try not to go in for soap boxes here. Just tell me your side of the story if you please.'

Well, he was just walking along with his dog Chas – had him since a puppy, great favourite with his youngest daughter was Chas. You oughter see the two of them together –

'Get on with it,' said the policeman, 'This isn't 'Appy Families.'

Well then – this youngster starts crying and carrying on. No, never seen him before. Was prepared to apologise handsomely to the officer who inadvertently got his eye in the way of his fist. Must have happened as he drew back his hand after this young rip bit it. To defend oneself when under attack was the right of any Englishman, *he* thought. No harm meant. Look – this very magnanimous – don't want to press charges. Give the boy a warning and let him go.

'You've got a nerve.' The desk officer opened another ledger and looked down its columns, 'King Charles spaniel, peke, Dandie Dinmont terrier – mean anything to you?'

Firm denial.

'What do you do – sell 'em again, hold 'em for ransom? All these dogs have been reported missing within the last few days. Now I don't want a dog thief on this patch. We've 'ad 'em before and we don't like 'em. They upset people. Turn out your pockets.'

There were further expostulations from the hard-faced gentleman whose countenance was growing blacker, further reiterations that he was a free-born Englishman. Eventually he gave way; there was nothing of interest but a messy, bloody parcel.

The policeman poked it with his pen.

'Liver.'

'My dinner. You can't lock a man up for carrying his dinner in his pocket!'

'I can. Get down you –' Chance had leapt up to the desk, whimpering and wagging his tail – 'Look at 'im. No wonder dogs find you irresistible. George!'

The police constable who had made the arrest stepped forward.

'Put 'im away, George. Then go and buy yourself a beefsteak for that eye. Oh, and George – tell that other gentleman that if 'e don't stop banging 'is 'ead I'll step inside and when I do I'll give 'im something to think about.'

Everyone melted away from the desk. The entertainment was over.

'Now then, young 'un.' The officer crooked his finger at Redemption, 'Tell us something about yourself. Yours is a face I never seen before.' He looked sharply at the boy, though not unkindly.

'Name? You got a name I suppose?' He wrote it down absently, as if from force of habit, 'From your tongue I should say you was from the North. Yorkshire?'

'Cumberland,' said Redemption, 'Wellshead is the town I come from.'

'Walked it did you?'

'Come on a ship.'

'Cabin boy? Sort of cabin boy? Well you either was or you wasn't.'

'I was put on it,' said Redemption, who thought he might as well tell the policeman all he wanted to know.

'Who put you on it?'

'Man called Jacob Slattery.'

'George! Come here George.' George had emerged again, dabbing at an eye that was fast closing, 'Wasn't Wellshead the place where 'is nibs come from? Ain't 'e head man up there?'

'Think it was,' said George, 'sure it was. Wellshead, Cumberland.'

'Where is 'e now? He might want to look at this young feller.'

'He went shopping,' said George. 'He's just about finished down here. Wanted some dress material for his wife.'

''Ee's a lad,' observed the officer. 'Wish 'e was our guv'nor. Hello – what's this?'

There was a commotion in the doorway. The policemen who were used to commotions and confident in their ability to deal with them regarded it with a detached interest.

'Let me through! Let me come through I say!'

The knot of people in the doorway burst aside as into the centre of the room staggered a slight figure whose spectacles were flashing with the light of battle.

'I leave the boy for an hour – less than an hour – and I find him snatched off the streets! Haven't you fellows anything better to do with your time?'

'Father Mulvanny.' The desk officer winked at George, 'So the young villain's a Roman?'

'He is not a villain!' snapped the priest, 'Nor is he a Catholic. But he is in my care.'

'And this is how you look after him?'

'Ach. I was at Feeney's – I was taking Feeney the Sacrament.'

'Feeney?' from George, 'Feeney the begging-letter writer? Well I never,' he shook his head and clicked his tongue, 'Feeney going home is he? That's a shame, I always liked Feeney.'

'Now then father,' said the desk officer, 'I want no quarrel with you. The boy is as innocent as a new-born lamb. Why don't you take him home, away from all the bad company that's to be found in here?'

'I suppose they're not a bad set of fellows,' said Father Mulvanny as they tramped home through a raw afternoon that smelt of fog, ''Tis a miserable vocation, to be always thinking the worst of everyone. However did ye get involved with the dog man?'

'He just come up and patted Chance,' said Redemption, 'I never expected he'd do 'owt else – then he hit me. Are there many like him in London?'

'What shall I say?' The priest frowned. 'Not fifty yards away are the wide streets and the big shops. Yet down that very alley –' he pointed down an area hung with old clothes where two or three dirty children crawled in the dust – 'Tuesday last a sailor slipped his knife into another's ribs and the poor man bled to death ten feet from where those babies play. This is the environment those poor unfortunates grow up in – and this is no rookery.'

The boy was puzzled. 'I'll say not. Pigeons and sparrows but no rooks. There isn't the wood for it.'

'The London rookeries need no trees,' said the priest grimly. 'But I'll tell you of the rookeries another day.'

They were outside his house; as they neared his door Father Mulvanny's mood switched. For no reason Redemption could see he winked and rubbed his hands together. 'I have been keeping a secret. Now come in will ye and see who we have sitting in front of the fire.'

Redemption was barely through the door before he found

himself seized and tossed into the air by a pair of brawny arms. He had a glimpse of tousled hair, the glint of an ear-ring and a set of broadly grinning teeth –

'Cropper! You've come! I knew you would, I knew you would . . .'

Cropper let out a burst of laughter and whirled him round again so that the room danced, before pulling him close in a bear hug.

Father Mulvanny watched through the open door.

'Look at the boy's face,' he murmured to Mrs O'Hare who had hurried from the kitchen at the noise, leaving the dinner to its own devices, 'Did you know he could smile? I did not believe the child had so much beauty in him. Why, Cropper has made an angel of him. See the dog bark and growl – little wonder, he's jealous.'

'I have been two days behind you all along,' said Cropper when they were all seated and he had filled in the main details of his adventures. 'I heard tell of you here and there.'

He ruffled the boy's hair and patted Chance with his free hand, his legs thrown out before the fire in that negligent, careless manner Redemption remembered so well. 'There was a widder-woman who claimed she bathed you before she fed you – is that right?'

'It's true,' said the boy, happily. 'She put me under the pump and the water were that cold it turned me blue and knocked the breath out of me. She said cleanliness were next to godliness and that was as near as I was ever ganna get.'

'Some said,' Cropper resumed, 'they had seen such a boy but with some poor half-starved long dog – no offence, old chap –.' To Chance, 'You was a good friend to Red when Cropper wasn't there. I will see you have a bone for that. I was never sure if it was you or not.'

'But what made the terrible mark on your head?'

Cropper touched his forehead, 'Belaying pin,' he said, modestly, 'I believe it would've killed a lesser man.'

'Ah well, your head is thick enough,' the priest said gravely.

'It was Locke who threw it,' Cropper said, ignoring the

comment, 'Locke or Mossop. It was Mossop who come forward to finish the job with his knife. I remember – just as he bent over me and the stink of his breath came wafting over his rotten teeth – I remember thinking how he used to stab his meat with it and thinking how he was about to use me the same way he used his dinner. Then the kind gentleman with the dogs shot him. The pair of us bled so bad you'd ha' thought they was killing a hog down on that snow.'

'What was the dogs called?' asked Redemption, whose mind was filled with the fight and the chase across the snow.

Cropper scratched his head. 'Blest if I know, Bite 'em and Rip I should think. The gentleman give them use of a cart to take Mossop away.

' "Stop your infernal squalling!' he says to him as they dumped him in it, "Thank your lucky stars I didn't aim for your vitals.' They sneaked away with their tails between their legs I can tell you.

'I was laid in the stable loft with two or three hunters down below for company – he was a devil to hunt, that man. A woman come along to bandage my head – an uncommon plain woman with fingers like saveloys – and all the little children come to peep in and then run away agin. I believe he told them I was a pirate. I lay up there the best part of three days weak as a baby. When the time come for me to go the gentleman give me a sovereign and said how he hated to see foul play – they give me no law, he said, no sporting chance. He was a sportsman that man was. He never did ask me what it was all about – though he did say it was his opinion there come a time when every man had to settle down. He was in a devilish lot of scrapes himself when he was younger, he said, but in the end he give it up.'

'Now there was a man of sense,' said Father Mulvanny, bending on Cropper the nearest he ever came to a glance of severity, and rising, 'However, we will come to your more personal affairs later. It is late. I will take a turn in my room and say my rosary. You will have much you wish to say to each other.'

'What do you think, Red?' Cropper asked seriously, when the door was closed, 'Did I oughter settle down?'

He looked so serious that the boy burst out laughing.

'No, it ain't no laughing matter Red. I done wrong to that girl running off the way I did. That's what I've been thinking – I ought to reform. All these tramping days I've been wondering how I could make it up to her. See –' Here he looked seriously at his feet – 'I love her. I was thinking I should marry her –' He glanced up in time to see an uneasy expression cross the boy's face.

'Not,' he said, ever so gently, 'that it would make any difference to me and you, Red. You're stuck with old Cropper –'

Just then came a smart rat-a-tat on the front door and an answering grumble from Mrs O'Hare, 'I might as well be the keeper of a lodging house for all the peace I get.'

'If it's Father Mulvanny you're wanting,' she cried, 'you can't see him. The poor dear man is at this very moment pacing his room saying his rosary to the Blessed Virgin – and him that spends every hour God sends tramping the streets like a coster's donkey. You must come back in the morning.'

'Not for the world, dear lady, would I disturb the reverend gentleman at his devotions. Heaven forfend! I will wait.'

The tones were somewhat better bred than those the lady was used to. Into the circle of gaslight swept a gentleman who raised his hat to her. A handsome, florid gentleman with side-whiskers, which he stroked as he beamed down on her.

'If you must,' she said, somewhat mollified, 'But 'tis a mighty prayerful heart he has in him. I have known him jabber away for a good two hours – God bless him for a saint – 'tis weary work waiting for him to have done.'

'I must speak with him tonight,' returned the gentleman, 'were he Saint Jerome himself.'

'This is the only room with a fire, your honour,' said Mrs O'Hare showing him into the sitting-room and signifying to Cropper and Redemption that they should give him room.

The gentleman put down the large brown paper parcel he carried and approached the fire.

'There is a fog,' he remarked cheerfully, 'don 't it make you cough? To tell you the truth I'm not used to London fog. Now then this is very fortunate –' He glanced over his shoulder to satisfy himself that the housekeeper had withdrawn. 'Not to disturb the reverend gentleman I'll be brief and come right to the point. It's not him I wish to see at all – it's a young man by the name of Redemption Greenbank. That, I take it, is yourself.' He turned his benign but sharp-eyed countenance on Redemption. The boy felt icy fingers lightly touch his spine.

'One moment, mister,' Cropper pushed himself between the stranger and Redemption, 'you make uncommon free with the boy's name. Perhaps you'd better tell us who you are.'

'I don't like your manners, friend,' said the strange gentleman politely, 'why don't you sit down?'

'As for that – if you don't like 'em, well, the street's outside. No one asked you to step in –'

'Cropper, Cropper, you will always be tearing at everything head on.' Father Mulvanny had entered the room, 'Why not take the thing the easy way round? Perhaps if we were to ask the gentleman politely he might tell us his name and the interest he has in the boy.' He advanced with his hand outstretched. 'I am Father Mulvanny. My housekeeper was so curious to know what the 'quality' were doing here instead of the usual beggars, tramps, paupers and suchlike trash – I use her words not mine – she broke into my prayers. Please be seated; what may we do for you?'

'I beg your pardon, sir,' said the gentleman, 'and yours too, young man – I am somewhat over-hasty myself these days. I believe it springs from frustration. I have had a difficult week or two. My name is Trumper – Inspector Trumper, I am a policeman – and I have been giving all my time to a particularly thorny case which despite all my best efforts has yielded nothing. Indeed –' he glanced at his parcel, '– I had all but given up and was preparing to go home. I do not belong to London, my domain is rather smaller. Wellshead –' He looked at Redemption, 'You come from there I believe? You are the boy whose dog was stolen?'

'Aye.'

Inspector Trumper nodded. 'The officer who spoke to you is a good man. He noted down one or two things besides - things of the utmost importance to me. A name. Jacob Slattery -' he hesitated, 'My investigation is a murder investigation. I have an uncommon interest in Mr Slattery. Anything you could tell me about him may be helpful, however small and trivial.'

'The killing in the cemetery?' demanded Cropper.

Trumper looked at him in some surprise. 'The killing in the cemetery. Yes.'

'Tell him, Red,' said Cropper, 'Go on - now's the time. Tell him.'

There was a silence. Redemption looked at them all; only Father Mulvanny was not looking at him. He sat with a hand shading his eyes looking into the fire.

'I can see you are afraid,' said Trumper, 'I promise I will treat what you tell me with confidentiality. You will be protected -'

'Slattery couldn't get me? He couldn't get me again?'

'Lord bless you - you need never see him.' Trumper's countenance did not betray the slightest trace of the rising excitement he was feeling. Here, at last, in the most unlikely of surroundings, was something!

'I was at McMurdo's,' said the boy, at length.

'A home for foundlings and orphans,' said Trumper to Father Mulvanny who raised his head.

'Aye. Well, they used to make us go to Mr Blaney's school. Some days I would not go -' Redemption shrugged and hurried on. Now he was started he would tell it all. 'At the back of the old burying ground there is an old gravedigger's hut. I used to go and set snares for there is a terrible lot of rabbits in them holes along the bank. When it rained I would sit in the hut, just doing nowt. Well, this day I am setting a snare, bending low down and getting it set right in the grass, so the rabbit won't see it, when I see a man come and sit on one of the old benches. It were Slattery though I nivver knew that then. All the days I ever came to the cemetery I've never seen one other person. Then – like he were a spirit or a goblin – another man appears. I nivver saw where he come from. He was just *there* – in the blink of an eye. As unlike Slattery as any man could be – ragged, dirty, hard. A bit like the man who took Chance but much worse – his face would give you nightmares.' He carefully told them all he could remember. Trumper's notebook was out and he was writing swiftly.

'Then, at the end, Slattery's face was all white and his eyes were like – sparks. He tossed down a coin and when t'other – Sol Rim – bent to pick it up he raised his stick like an axe and

Redemption took a deep breath, 'when it come down I pushed my face into the grass so I mayn't see. But I could hear – blow after blow, like a madman chopping wood. When I looked up there was blood splashed on the stone and Slattery was *smiling*! I run away from it and that night I telt Mrs Biggs . . .'

He carried on quickly until the story was done.

When it was over no one spoke for a moment.

'I'll smoke a cigar if I may,' Inspector Trumper said.

Cropper grasped Redemption by the shoulder, 'It's better told, Red. Now the police know they can begin to come down on this Slattery!'

Father Mulvanny had begun to pace the room. Behind his spectacles his eyes seemed old and tired.

'This is a devilish dirty business, Reverend,' said the Inspector, at length.

'I see enough sin,' returned the priest, 'I walk its highways and by the Lord's good grace I keep a merry heart. But the sins that go hard with me are those against the children. Truly, it would be better for this man Jacob Slattery that a millstone were hung about his neck and he cast into the sea. That is Christ's judgement, not mine.'

'But we have no evidence that he meant the boy to die.'

'Did he not throw his life away among thieves? Is not the sending to Australia a death sentence? Ach – and the treachery of the woman!'

'Mrs Biggs? A cold woman. I can't bear cold women. It will give me a great deal of pleasure to lock her up.'

Father Mulvanny knelt at Redemption's feet and took the boy's hands between his own, 'So this was the burden you carried all those long miles? God forgive me for thinking you did not have a smile in you! And it was Cropper who stood by you?'

'Aye. When there was no one else and no one would help me.'

'I was planning to come sharp with you about the young woman in Liverpool.' The priest took hold of Cropper's shaggy head and shook it gently, 'Well, ye've took the wind from my sails.' He went to the door, 'I feel the need for a restorative – the only drink we have in the house is the altar wine – I'll go and ask Mrs O'Hare for the keys.'

'Now,' said Trumper, wincing slightly as the first sip of wine passed his lips, 'I can have Slattery arrested at once merely by telegraphing my people in Wellshead. But I wish the case against him to be as strong as possible. Redemption's evidence should be all we need but you have no idea how an experienced counsel may twist and turn things –' He paused, catching a low muttered word from Cropper, 'You are quite right – gammon. A good lawyer could gammon the boy out of countenance – "I put it to you Redemption Greenbank that this whole story is a tissue of lies born solely out of the malice you harbour towards your former benefactor" – that sort of thing, casting doubts on what is plain and flatly contradicting the highly probable –'

'We thought, Redemption and me,' broke in Cropper, 'of going down to Putney where this Slattery was married.'

Inspector Trumper waved this away, 'I've been. I discovered Slattery's wife had a sister who still lives there. She hates Jacob Slattery but hatred don't amount to evidence in a court of law – not unless you're trying to prove a motive.'

'There's the written confession Sol Rim spoke of,' suggested Father Mulvanny.

'Exactly. There are two questions here. First, does it exist? Second, how do we lay hands on it?'

Father Mulvanny looked thoughtful. 'That may not be so difficult after all. Redemption has remembered some very significant details. This man lived in the Seven Dials?'

'Aye – with a woman.'

'I never heard of him myself,' said the priest, rubbing his chin, 'but the Seven Dials is only a small area. Someone must know Sol Rim and the woman he lived with.'

'He said she run off every time he was away,' Redemption put in.

'We can't blame her for that,' said the priest. 'But the house they lived in can't run away and this document may be hidden there.'

'I'm afraid there's one great difficulty, Reverend,' interposed Inspector Trumper. 'Namely that the police are most definitely *non grata* in the Seven Dials. Why, the place is one of the worst rookeries in London. We can't just walk over there and ask after Sol Rim as we would anywhere else. No one would give us a straight answer. They tell me it's a brave policeman who walks there alone. *I* wouldn't.'

'They sometimes need a priest. I have been there on several occasions when some poor Irishman has reached his end. Even there, in squalor and sin, men seek forgiveness – even there. I have one or two good friends in the Seven Dials, Inspector Trumper. I will find out where Sol Rim lived.' He turned to the boy. 'We talked today of rookeries, Redemption. Rookeries where there are no trees. Well, the Seven Dials is such a place and a man may be picked clean there as well as anywhere else. If we go there remember this; no matter how bad the people appear to be or how they live, a determined effort by their betters – the rich who have made this capital city the capital of the world – could clear it out in a month. Aye, and find them all somewhere decent to live and give them honest jobs.'

'My, you are quite the radical,' Trumper said mockingly.

Father Mulvanny thrust out his jaw. 'I am a priest,' he said.

ELEVEN

Cropper began to reform the very next day by going to Mass. He offered to show Redemption the 'ropes' and took him with him. Redemption liked it. He liked the smell, the ranks of candles before the crudely-coloured statues, the red sanctuary lamp. He even liked the statues themselves, pious representations of the Virgin and Child and the Sacred Heart were works of high art to him.

Once they were in their bench Cropper heaved a great sigh, indicative of a man laying down a burden, and buried his face in his hands. His silent meditations lasted only a few moments before being succeeded by a series of jaw-breaking yawns. He winked at Redemption and confided that he hadn't 'been for a bit'. After this he went to sleep.

Redemption enjoyed the quiet and sense of mystery. Father Mulvanny, dressed in a rich purple so unlike his everyday shabbiness the boy had difficulty recognising him, poured out prayer after impassioned prayer in Latin, now with his hands raised, now busily pouring water and wine into the chalice, now raising something to Heaven. The old women clicked their beads or mumbled to themselves while Redemption's spirit suddenly broke free and soared within himself.

He couldn't have said what happened. Only that he had escaped from the stifling, narrow world of McMurdo's, escaped safely from death. Cropper and Father Mulvanny had given him life and now, in a manner he could not understand, were enriching it. He was not aware of how arid his life had been, how starved of love, of companionship, of fancy or laughter. All he knew was that at this moment he seemed to have taken flight, to be at once looking down on this small chapel and the busy figure of Father Mulvanny offering Mass while at the same time kneeling there small and alone before the Almighty.

Later that afternoon Father Mulvanny informed them he had the address they sought. Inspector Trumper, beaming with triumph and good fellowship met them near Redemption's old haunt, Covent Garden.

'I have a blackjack in my pocket,' he said, 'It does wonders for a fellow's self-confidence.'

'There will be no fighting,' said Father Mulvanny, 'Where is it ye imagine ye're going? If we keep together no one will meddle with us.'

He led them into a proliferation of poor streets no different from any other such warren in the capital. Perhaps there were more than the usual number of idlers and loungers to watch them pass, perhaps there were more than the usual number of drinking-places. Father Mulvanny led them through it all with a nod and a smile for anyone who caught his eye, undaunted by ill looks or contempt.

At length he drew up before a house no different from any other as regards its state of dilapidation but ornamented with a small man with red hair and only one eye. As he didn't offer to move, he was sitting in the doorway, or make any other attempt at communication, they picked their way over him, Inspector Trumper doffing his hat with one hand while toying with his blackjack with the other. He drew back, 'Do all the houses smell like this, Reverend?'

The priest ignored him, consulting a scrap of paper.

' 'Tis an upstairs room. The woman still lives there and she had a message this morning to say we would be calling.'

Inspector Trumper was astonished, 'Good Lord, the Metropolitan Force could use a man with your contacts, Father.'

'Ach, I met a fellow yesterday who knows the house. He carried a message for me; that's all there is to it.'

They clattered up the bare staircase and came to a room where a woman, no longer young, was throwing articles of clothing onto a cloth spread on the floor.

'Walk in,' she said, 'make yourself at home. I'm off.'

'I'm Father Mulvanny – ye had a message from me?'

She paused, staring at him, one hand on her hip.

'Who are you to be sending me messages? Is it true?'

'It is.'

She laughed without mirth. 'I'll be honest – it's the best news I've heard since he got drunk and fell down and broke his arm. I wished it had been his neck. I'm glad he's dead – I hated him.' Her eyes narrowed, 'Here – it ain't a trick is it?'

''Tis the gospel truth.'

'He's been away longer than this afore now. He's always going away and coming back viler than ever. Hitting me about the room. He was a prize, my Sol was.'

'This gentleman has seen his body.'

Inspector Trumper stepped forward, 'Er, Sol Rim lived here?'

Her lip curled, 'What've I just been saying? We lived here together and when he wasn't hitting me he was boasting how we was going to be rich – rich! What did he look like?'

'I beg your pardon?'

'When he was dead.' She laughed again in a wild way, 'Did he make a pretty corpse?'

'Madam, death is no fit subject for levity. Your husband was cruelly murdered, have you no compassion in you – no womanly feeling? Can you spare no thought for him.'

She was crying. 'Not for him,' she muttered, biting her lip with violence. 'For me, for my life, what has it been? What do you all want, poking and staring?'

'Justice,' said Father Mulvanny, 'justice for your husband, for an innocent murdered woman, for this boy.'

She glanced down at Redemption. Something in his face seemed to soften her. 'What do you want?'

'Did he ever mention a written confession he had in his possession?'

'No.'

'If he had a paper, a document, where would he keep it?'

She indicated a small chest, like a seaman's chest, in the corner.

'That's all he had. He kept it locked. Even now I'm half-afraid to touch it, he never liked his things touched. I was going to take it to the dolly shop and see what he'd give me for it unopened.'

Inspector Trumper dragged it into the light.

'You would have had a struggle, madam,' he said, panting.

'You can have it for two pound. I'll have to find work. I need money.'

'I'm a policeman,' said the inspector, looking about, 'as we haven't brought a jemmy with us I'll trouble you for the loan of your hat pin, ma'am.'

She handed it to him wonderingly.

'Cropper, be a good fellow and hold my coat.'

In his shirtsleeves Inspector Trumper looked like an eminent medical man about to perform a dissection in front of his students.

'Reverend sir, gentlemen, madam. It is a common saying, is it not, that a chain is only as strong as its weakest link.'

'Yes, sir.'

'Thank you, Cropper. This is a fine chest, bound with iron studded with brass, but it illustrates the truth of that observation. The padlock is old-fashioned and easy to pick. The art of picking locks - in an elementary fashion of course - is something I learned at public school. I used to steal cocoa and brew it illicitly. Horrible stuff.' While he spoke Inspector Trumper was testing the pin in the lock, easing it this way and that. 'I still entertain my daughters by allowing them to lock me in the cupboard under the stairs, they think I'm terribly clever ... I must confess that the peace and quiet is so restful that I often take longer than I ought getting out ... once they forgot me altogether and went out shopping with their mama ... ah.' With another manipulation the lock was sprung, 'Here we are.'

They all drew closer to see what the chest held.

The detritus of a wasted life: a shirt, a crowbar, two silver

candlesticks, some loose coin, a knife, a pack of playing cards, a flask.

Inspector Trumper handed the candlesticks to Cropper. 'We'll have those. I'll take my oath they came from Slattery's home in Putney – I've read their description often enough this week, they'll make useful exhibits in his trial. Here –' to the woman, 'you may take the money and the other things, you should be able to get something for them. What's this –'

He fished out a greasy wallet from the depths of the chest and from it drew a cracked and grimy sheet of paper.

'Hallo ... dated and signed by William – is it William? – Bowers, "being on my death bed and wishing to die free ..." Great Scott this is it! Listen – "I did murder Sarah Slattery of Putney" on such and such a date, can't make it out, "I done the deed with one other." We all know who that was, this is the part we want, just listen to this – "Her husband Jacob Slattery paid us to do it, leaving a window open so we could get in easy –"'

'Gentlemen, Slattery is as good as convicted. He can't wriggle out of this, not if he had ten lawyers. Our friend Sol Rim left no detail out. The whole thing is witnessed by him and someone else, 'Irene Short' – a woman, is that you?'

'No,' said the woman. 'She's dead. She was afore me.'

A beam of triumph had overspread Inspector Trumper's features.

'There is no more to be done. Gentlemen, our case is complete.'

On the way back to his hotel Inspector Trumper discussed train times. The whole journey to Wellshead would take up the best part of two days. They were too late for today's trains but it was agreed that Cropper and Redemption should accompany him back to Wellshead on the first train of the morning. Father Mulvanny, of course, remained where he was.

'And glad to,' he said. 'Glad to, I have no taste for this police work. 'Tis only lifting stones to see what crawls beneath.'

'At least have dinner at my hotel, Reverend. It's the least I can do to repay you. Without your aid this business would be far from over.'

He would do that. The Inspector promised the best the menu could offer. Before going in for dinner he asked if there were any messages for him. There was.

'Bad news, Inspector?'

He shrugged. 'My men didn't make their arrest. Slattery is gone.'

TWELVE

The day of Inspector Trumper's first meeting with Redemption was the day of Slattery's disappearance.

That morning Factor raised the matter which had gnawed at him for days. He stood dogged, keeping calm only with an effort, repeating his question.

'When wilt thoo go?'

'Soon . . . soon,' Slattery against the cushions watching the fire, his eyes creased for want of sleep. He slept, he supposed, but had no memory of it, his life was become one long, waking dream.

'Ye've gone daft!'

Slattery let his eyes flicker to where his servant stood clenching and unclenching his hands.

'Thoo's telt no one thoo's off. I know that for a fact.'

Slattery regarded his servant; it was strange but, in his odd way, Factor was attached to him.

'I'm ill, Factor. You are daily witness to the changes in me. I can't sleep and during the day I see . . .'

Factor swung his arm angrily. 'See! What does thoo see?'

'People who are dead,' Slattery drew the covering closer about his shoulders.

'Ghosts!'

'No, there are no ghosts,' said Slattery, after an interval, watching the manic leap of the flames. 'Only the phantasms of a sick brain and . . . evil.'

Factor was wordless. His life was slipping away because his master was daft, going to Ireland, shutting up the big house and fleeing as if the place was the nightly haunt of goblins and demons. Cracked. And he, Factor, would suffer.

'Sometimes I fancy I can see evil, Factor, swirling in the air like particles, white particles, like ash,' said Slattery, looking at the fire, 'a sick fancy.'

'A doctor –'

'A doctor can't cure me. I need a change – a break from old associations.' He didn't add that since the boy had escaped he was in daily peril. Such is the instinct to preserve life that, sick as he undoubtedly was, Slattery was capable of decisive action.

Where had it all begun? When his wife was murdered? Evil was there before then; love of money, love of power, love of self. He had suppressed the canker all these years until Sol Rim had come back from the past. It was a contract; once it was entered into every subsequent clause must be met. Sol Rim had to die. He should have killed the boy too, and the woman, Mrs Biggs.

'Have you ever thought, Factor,' he went on, still watching the posturing, antic flames, 'how one act can make a prisoner of you? Redemption . . . there is no redemption.'

Here was something Factor could get hold of. 'What act? What art thoo driving at? Is it summat to do with that lad we kept locked up? The one thoo told me had gone to Australia –'

'He's safe enough.' He was safe. He was escaped, there was no telling when the blow would fall.

'I warn thee, master – ' Factor was not satisfied.

'Warn me! You warn me!' There was some return to Slattery's old manner. He gazed bleakly at his servant before turning away. 'Get my things ready. I will go out directly.'

They both knew he had nowhere to go. Or rather, that all his aimless wanderings tended in the same direction bringing him to the crazy gate of the old cemetery. If Factor could have seen him then he would have been even more deeply disturbed. Slattery's features worked themselves into a fearful grimace as he stared into the depths of the cemetery. It was as if he was making faces.

But Factor never saw. Every evening he watched for the return of the dark figure of his master. For company he had always the reflection that his secure life in the big house was shortly to end. He looked out over the lawns, over to the grey sea, clenching and unclenching his hands.

Slattery's plans were complete. The *Lord Henry* was ready to sail. He took only the clothes he wore, his bag of money, a small revolver, and his evil, poisoned heart.

Slattery was gone. As trees and hedges rushed by his carriage window all Trumper could see was Slattery rushing headlong away from him. Slattery gone. The *Lord Henry* was still in port but it was surely too obvious a place to hide. Was he to have his moment of triumph snatched away while all Wellshead laughed and said Trumper bungled it?

Slattery gone. He listened to Cropper, shouting something to Redemption above the engine noise, something about a girl, Liverpool, Father Mulvanny, a letter he had written, marriage. Normally it was the sort of topic to interest him but marriage made him think of Slattery. Everything was Slattery. He looked at Redemption and thought of Slattery looming over him, he looked out of the window and saw Slattery rushing away over fields and ditches, past startled cattle and staring yokels. The rails took it up as their refrain, 'Slattery gone, Slattery gone'. His package for his wife and daughters lay unheeded at his feet. Slattery had a wife once. Slattery gone. Slattery gone.

He took out his watch. Another four hours. Four more hours for Slattery.

It was afternoon before the train reached Wellshead. They sniffed the damp sea air and great clouds of steam from the engine waiting for the sergeant to finish his report.

It wasn't much. No sign of Slattery anywhere, no word at his home or office. The man Factor told them Slattery was going to Ireland but there had been no sailings from Wellshead. They had contacted Liverpool but no passengers answering to his description had crossed from there. Factor also told them some tale of a boy locked in the attic and shipped aboard the *Lord Henry* at night. Oh yes, the *Lord Henry* was in port loading coals.

'Have you the warrant we need to search her?'

'As soon as you telegraphed, sir.'

'Good man, three men will do the job adequately though I doubt we'll find anything. Oh, and sergeant – this is the boy from the attic. I'll explain on the way to the docks.'

The *Lord Henry* was moored under the coal chute where waggon after waggon shed its load with a rumble and a clanging of couplings. The dust was intense but even in the mingling of dock labourers Cropper recognised Spavin.

'Take Redemption and stay out of sight,' advised Trumper. 'Slattery is our concern now. We don't want to be troubled with anything else.'

They sat in the lee of the harbour wall stroking Chance.

'I've seen so many drinking marriages,' said Cropper taking up his theme again, thinking to divert the boy's mind from Slattery. 'It worries me. Father Mulvanny says I must do it if I love the girl. He says I must put her above all others and steer clear of wild company – then we will be blessed. He says that it is ruin to think of yourself all the time. Father Mulvanny says it ain't poverty that makes people bad but selfishness. It's just that poor people get caught sooner. He says if I learn to be thinking of other people, to be looking after other people, we'll be all right.'

He looked anxiously at Redemption.

'We know what it's like don't we, Red? Not to have nobody. I don't want any child of mine on the streets because his daddy run away or took to drink.'

'Aye,' Redemption didn't like this talk of Cropper marrying. It meant he would go away again.

'Father Mulvanny said another thing,' Cropper's voice was gentle. 'He said we need each other, you and me. He said if my girl was agreeable – and she will be – we should offer you a home with us. He said it would do me good to have you to look after as well.' Cropper was too delicate to point out that Redemption had no home. 'It would be doing me a kindness, you would be keeping me on the straight and narrow, like.'

It was agreed, not without a certain dumb emotion from

Redemption which filled his heart and made him blink rapidly.

'Does she like dogs?' he asked. 'Could Chance come as well? I could never give him up.'

'Dogs? Why she dotes on 'em!' exclaimed Cropper, who in truth had no idea of his affianced bride's feelings in the matter. 'There would allus be a corner for old Chance. Aye, and a bone every day of his life!'

Cropper took the boy by the shoulders. He felt older. That moment marked another stage in their relationship.

At the *Lord Henry* Trumper was growing increasingly fretful. He ground his cigar under his heel and fumed silently.

'It's no go, sir.' His sergeant, red in the face, covered in coal dust. 'Slattery's not on her – unless he's buried under four ton of coal.'

'What about the master?'

'Man named Sully – though for my money Spavin is in charge – a drinker I'd say. He doesn't deny he carried the boy, Slattery paid the passage. He says the boy was to be met in London. Knows nothing of any trip to Australia.'

'Of course he doesn't.'

'Another thing – they've finished loading and the tide's running. He wants to be off.'

'What do you think, sergeant?'

'Let her go. I'll take my oath Slattery isn't there. To be honest we can't stop her.'

They watched from the quayside as the hatches were battened and the *Lord Henry* slipped her cable. Spavin grinned openly at them from the bridge.

'The oaf,' muttered Trumper. 'For two pins I'd knock his head against his own mainmast. Do you think they know where Slattery is?'

'They can't pick him up without us knowing. We've men at all the ports.'

'I wish I was as sure, sergeant. I can't help feeling Slattery's outwitted us. Where the devil could he have got to? How does he eat, travel, rest? Have there been no reports at all?'

'None, sir. It's plain he's in hiding hereabouts - he can't have gone far. As you say, someone must have seen him.'

'Well, we must begin to search. I suppose I'd better go home - how did my wife take the news of my disappearance?'

'Handsome woman, your wife, sir. She was very composed - not a tear.'

'That's all you know, sergeant. Be a good man and come and rescue me after an hour - I'll take Redemption and Cropper. That will give the women something to fuss over.'

Inspector Trumper was in great depression of spirits as he got into his carriage. There was no smile for Redemption, no caress for Chance. He told the driver the direction and turned his face away, watching the *Lord Henry* navigate the harbour mouth.

They had not gone very far before his thoughts were disturbed by an urgent rapping at the window.

'We've got something, sir.'

It was a memorandum from the police station. A farm worker had come in to report he had seen a glimmer of light from one of the caves on Fleswick beach for the past few nights. He thought it was smugglers. Fleswick was a rocky haven two miles on the other side of the headland from Wellshead. No one used it, the only land access was by a steep and narrow footpath, the waters were full of hidden rocks. It had this one advantage; so steeply did the sea bed slope away from the land that a skilful pilot could bring a medium-sized craft almost to the shore. It was a natural smugglers' haven.

Trumper crumpled the paper.

'Of course. Slattery's waiting at Fleswick.'

They looked at the *Lord Henry* almost on the horizon now. Once out of sight she would change her tack and make round the headland to pick up Slattery.

It was Redemption who broke the silence first.

'The top path!'

A footpath ran from the harbour like a ribbon over the cliff tops and into Fleswick.

'Sergeant!' bawled Trumper.

He outlined what had happened. He would take Cropper – and Redemption who wouldn't be left – along the cliff path. The other way to Fleswick across country was left for the sergeant to cut off Slattery's retreat.

'We'll be slower,' warned the sergeant. 'Are you sure you and Cropper can manage him?'

Inspector Trumper was already running. 'Slattery's an old woman,' he called, 'I'm more worried the *Lord Henry* will get there first!'

Spavin had told him about the caves. Echoing, restless caves where the sand was damp and water drained from the fields above. There was no rest in them as there was no rest in anything else. They were cold, he had been cold and wet for days.

Jacob Slattery, fugitive, hair plastered to his head with wet, coat flapping in the wind as he watched and waited for the *Lord Henry*. His eyes strained with watching, sunken for lack of sleep, the once smooth cheeks disfigured by a three days' growth of bread.

Ranged before him on one of the giant rocks that broke out of the sea were a party of sea birds, waiting likewise. One of them, all in black like himself, dried its wings as it waited, turning its head to reveal a long murderous beak like a knife. That bird was like himself, he thought, touching the dead weight of the pistol in his pocket, respectable, murderous.

What was he that he should run like this? It was his fancy that even the dumb animals, the sheep, turned their backs when he passed them along the cliff path. It was the wind and rain that made them turn, he knew, but the fancy remained. He was shunned and unwanted. It was in the wind that buffeted him, in the gulls that mocked above his head, in the rain that stung his skin. It would have been better to fling himself from the cliff instead of hurrying by. Perhaps he would find oblivion in the rocky sea that crept flatly below. He could imagine the moment, imagine hanging in the air like a gull before plunging down in one long scream of release. But he would not. They could not drive him to it, he would rather kill first. Trumper, any of them.

A boy had fallen from these cliffs in the spring, after gulls' eggs. He turned to look up at the cliffs again, the gulls on the ledges, staining the sandstone white with their droppings. Four hundred feet he fell, they said, dead before he hit the ground. A comfortable notion. How did they know, the fools?

The cloud was thickening, grey and milky, the sea and horizon blending so that it was impossible to say where one ended and the other began. He strained outward once more trying to make out the shape of the *Lord Henry*. Spavin would come, he would do most things for money.

The birds ranged on the rock took to flight. The black bird with the cruel beak flying over his head, its short wings flapping hurriedly, the long neck stretched out. Did they see something he did not?

At that moment a dog barked.

He raised his head abruptly. Coming down into the cove were a small party with a dog that capered and barked about their feet. Soon they would be on the beach. There was something in their bearing which made him study them closely; two men, the smaller figure of a child, the dog. He knew that stout figure at the head of the party. By all the devils in hell he knew the child too. He turned back to the sea, glassy and oily, empty of any aid. They were come for him, for his life.

At once Slattery dropped his bag and made a run for the southern cliff. Just as one path brought you into Fleswick from Wellshead another rose to take you away southward, up the cliff again and along the tops. It was no more than a sheep track, greasy with the rain. He slipped and the red earth made a great streak like a gash of blood along his thigh.

They were clattering along the pebbles now, shouting at him, 'In the name of the law!' Trumper probably. Things were too late for Law now. The path was sheer, he had to scrabble with his hands and knees for purchase, sending down shower after shower of small pebbles. Already he was clammy with sweat, taking his breath in great laboured gulps. They would not take him, not if he could reach the cliff top.

He slipped again, sending more pebbles into the faces of his pursuers who had strung out behind him, Trumper in the lead, coatless, Cropper and the boy behind, Chance dancing somewhere in the short tufted grass, barking excitedly, enjoying this glorious game.

Slattery had almost attained the cliff top, he was standing, leaning himself forward, tearing up clods of turf to cast down on them.

He was there, the yawning drop and the creeping sea two yards to his right. If he looked down he could see where he had been waiting, the dark speck which was his bag lying where it had been dropped. The wind whipped at his coat turning him to ice as he gulped each greedy breath. Two steps, two little steps would set him free, put eternity between himself and his pursuers. Yet even as he prepared for death his body strained for life, his heart pumped, his lungs sucked in draught after draught of air, his brain sent impulses to his limbs. It was ironic. He stepped forward.

'No – !'

He turned. Through his failing sight, through the swirling particles that filled his vision like falling snow, he saw his enemy, Trumper. Trumper, bareheaded and coatless, bathed in perspiration, his honest face pleading, one arm raised in a gesture of supplication.

'I beg you –'

Well. His death would cost a life.

He took out the revolver cold and heavy from his pocket. He cocked the hammer.

'No – Slattery – !'

As the sound of the shot battered about the cliffs Trumper's mouth formed itself into an 'ah' of surprise. He staggered back as if struck a heavy blow, back with all his weight into Cropper who attempted too late to escape his falling body. The pair of them slithered away to the bottom of the path in an incongruous tangle of arms and legs which would have been funny in another context.

It was funny now. He laughed, from his eyes shone the deathly arrogance which had consumed his life, he suffered no one to stand against him, even now.

From the mists of the sea he could make out the shape of the *Lord Henry*. Too late; Spavin would never take his money now. Across the fields and along the path behind came hurrying dark figures, more of them, they hemmed him in. Too late, too late.

'Red! Make a run for it!'

He glanced down. The boy was staring up at him, his pale young face intent, unable to move. The dog crouched on its belly beside him in the grass, shivering. He had meant the boy no harm.

He raised the revolver again.

'Redemption . . .' He wanted to explain why he was going to kill him. Even through the swirling mists of his sight the intent, innocent young gaze troubled him. His wife must have looked this way at the end, the very end.

'Ah . . . .' He stepped back, shaking his head, trying to rid himself of the impression that the figure on the grass was a young woman. It couldn't be. His wife was gazing up at him.

'No – !'

Sol Rim grinned at him.

With a low growl the dog leapt for him, his snapping jaws fastening on his throat.

Another shot hammered and battered the cliffs. From every ledge and perch the gulls rose up like a blizzard, filling the echoing air with their keening and crying. They whirled upwards, rising along the cliff-tops as the contagion of alarm spread until the sky was clouded with wheeling and floating birds.

No shot succeeded. At length they grew quieter and gradually began to seek their rocky perches once more. At length the sound of their calling gave way to the wind that whipped the grass along the cliff paths, to the sea that broke on the pebbles.

Cropper, besmeared in red mud, was first on the scene.

Redemption was alone, still crouching in the grass where he and Chance had lain. Of Slattery and the dog there was no sign. The wind stirred the grass where he had stood, the sea lay flat and empty.

Into Cropper's head came the words Father Mulvanny had used – ... 'It would be better for him that a millstone were hanged about his neck and he cast into the sea'. Well, the dog had been his millstone.

He glanced down at Redemption.

'You give him his life once. He's paid you back now.'

By the time he had carried the shivering boy down the greasy path Trumper's men had arrived and begun to attend their chief. Trumper lay among the rocks, bruised and bleeding, his head pillowed on someone's coat, nursed by his devoted sergeant.

'How are you, sir?' Cropper stopped by him with his burden.

'Nothing to worry about, Cropper. The bullet took me in the shoulder. I'm more apprehensive about what my wife will say ...' He attempted a weak laugh, 'This is my best shirt. How is Redemption?'

Cropper looked down at him tenderly.

'I think his heart is broke,' he said.